W
AND TH

YOUNG AMERICAN PATRIOTS
BOOK ONE

WILL NORTHAWAY &
THE QUEST FOR LIBERTY

SUSAN OLASKY

CROSSWAY BOOKS

A DIVISION OF
GOOD NEWS PUBLISHERS
WHEATON, ILLINOIS

Will Northaway and the Quest for Liberty

Copyright © 2004 by Susan Olasky

Published by Crossway Books

        a division of Good News Publishers

        1300 Crescent Street

        Wheaton, Illinois 60187

Cover design: David LaPlaca

Cover illustration: Thomas LaPadula

First printing 2004

Printed in the United States of America

Library of Congress Cataloging-in-Publication Data
Olasky, Susan,
  Will Northaway and the quest for liberty / Susan Olasky.
    p. cm.
  Summary: Accused of a crime he did not commit, Will leaves
England for America, where his search for his long-lost father becomes
entangled with the pre-Revolutionary turmoil of the colonies' feud
with England.
  ISBN 1-58134-475-9 (TPB)
  1. United States—History—Colonial period, ca. 1600-1775—Juvenile
fiction. [1. United States—History—Colonial period, ca. 1600-1775—
Fiction. 2. Fathers and sons—Fiction.] I. Title.
PZ7.O425Wi   2004
[Fic]—dc22   2003025425

CH		14	13	12	11	10	09	08	07	06	05	04
15	14	13	12	11	10	9	8	7	6	5	4	3	2	1

For Ben

ONE

Fog shrouded the stone piers of London Bridge, hugging the brick buildings and veiling the wooden shop signs creaking on their rusty chains: Four Brushes, Cork Jacket, Ye Golden Fleece, Lamb and Breeches.

Will Northaway pulled his linsey-woolsey vest closer about his skinny chest. He wiped his sleeve across his dripping nose and sniffled. The boy wasn't much to look at, standing just over four and a half feet tall. His skin was sallow and covered with scabs that never seemed to heal. His clothes were patched and patched again, until the fabric was worn so thin that there was nothing to sew a patch to. He looked up at the signs above him, and his eye caught a glimpse of letters peeking out from the fog: Ye Go. The boy laughed bitterly. *Go where?* he wondered.

No one called the boy Will. He was known as Fish—that's what he'd always been called. Perhaps it was because he hung around the wharves so much, begging for fish scraps. Or maybe it was the smell coming from the scraps that he carried in his pocket as insurance against a hungry stomach.

Sometimes when the air was particularly bad—when the fog and the soot left a damp layer of ash on the streets, walks, and windows—the boy would huddle in a doorway or a dry corner in a tavern.

"Joe Tinker," he'd call, "how about a pint, and I'll wash yer windows."

More often than not, Joe Tinker or Edwin Gaunt or Thad Buxton would give the scrawny kid a pint of ale. Will would halfheartedly run a grimy rag over the sooty windows and then run off. And by the time he came again to ask for a drink or a bite, the tavern keeper would have forgotten his last pitiful effort.

Everyone up and down High Street knew Will. He'd steal fruit, but never from the same vendor twice in a week. He'd swipe a piece of leather to sell, but not the best piece. Was it pity that caused people to overlook his crimes? Perhaps. But it may have been acceptance. Thousands of orphaned children roamed London and Southwark, looting their way through life. They were a scourge to hardworking folks, and people had no pity on most of them.

But Will Northaway was different. Ever since he was a baby, hardly able to toddle down the dank streets, neighbors had taken pity on him. They never expected him to survive, and when he did, they regarded him as something akin to a good luck charm. If Will Northaway could make it in Southwark, maybe they could as well. Will had long ago figured out that they'd scream and scold if he stole from them, but no one had ever reported him to the law. And so he prowled the streets of Southwark as if it were his own territory, and God protect any scalawag who wandered onto Will's turf.

So it was that one wet June day when folks huddled close to their fires, Will covered himself with a bit of blanket and huddled outside the door of Buxton's Tavern. As long as he didn't block the folks coming in or going out, the barkeep didn't bother him. It was past noon, and time hung heavy on Will. He'd been up since dawn, and so as he sat on the damp walk, his scratchy blanket thrown over his head, he shut his eyes and dozed off to sleep.

Just then a ragtag band of boys ran down the street, kicking a pebble. Their laughter woke Will, and he watched as they tipped over a peddler's cart and startled an old woman begging on the corner. The pebble skipped over the rough cobblestones and splashed in the muck that filled the gutter at the center of the street. When a carriage going too fast rumbled around the corner, its wheel hit the gutter, sending a spray of mud into the air and over the boys. Like terriers after a rat, the boys chased the carriage, hurling outraged insults and pebbles at it with equal energy. One of the rocks missed the carriage and hit Will Northaway's forehead.

He sprang to his feet, throwing off his blanket and grabbing a stone. He knew if he didn't defend himself against these intruders, no one else would, and they would take over his streets. He charged out of the doorway, chucking rocks at the surprised boys before turning and dashing down an alleyway.

"After him," they yelled, scooping up more pebbles and taking off in pursuit. Will had the advantage because he knew every alley and lane off Borough High Street. He also knew the taverns where soldiers liked to drink. He led his attackers on a merry chase before ducking into a tiny alley behind an inn called the Porridge Pot.

The boys, still yelling, stopped abruptly in front of the inn. A handful of red-coated soldiers outside the tavern door turned at the noise. "What's going on here?" the leader demanded. "Causing more trouble, are you? We'll put you out of business for a while. We'll give you reasons not to come back."

Will peeked out from his hiding place and waved to the boys before trotting off, laughing as he imagined the trouble they faced. Wet from the steady drizzle, he suddenly became aware of a fierce hunger. He hadn't eaten since breakfast when he'd had a stale bun—part of some gentleman's supper dropped carelessly in the street. By habit his hand dug in his pocket where he found some crumbs, a penny given to him by someone, and a few odd raisins. The penny would buy him a pint of ale perhaps or a piece of yesterday's meat pie. He'd better get to the wharves, he thought. He could still find some fish if he hurried.

Peddlers, done for the day, had parked their wagons at the side of the street, forcing other wagons and carriages to the center where they couldn't avoid the gutter. Mud sprayed up constantly, spattering storefronts and anyone unlucky enough to be standing in front of them. There were no sidewalks; so people on foot did their best to avoid the carriages and the occasional bow-front windows or stairways that jutted out unexpectedly into the street.

Will darted in and out of traffic. More than one coach driver threatened him with an upraised whip, but he ignored them all. In the marketplace the air was ripe with the smell of rotting apples and other fruit. Will slowly eased over to a wagon where a peddler was busy weighing out lemons for a loud woman in a flounced dress. As the peddler collected her money, the boy grabbed two apples and stuffed them into his pocket. He didn't run but instead pretended to be examining the other fruits and nuts, all the while inching away.

The peddler caught sight of him. "Go on! Get away from my cart, Will Northaway," she screeched.

He grinned at her. "Are you going to chase me, Granny?"

"You're a wicked boy. But you'll get yours, you will. A day will come."

Will was up the street by then. He made a mocking bow as he sauntered away, waiting to bite into the apple ∗il she was no longer watching. It was one thing to tease the an, but it was another to taunt her with the proof.

When he figured he was far enough away, he reached into his pocket and found that he had done well. The apple didn't even have a worm hole.

Four bites, and nothing remained but the core. Two more bites, and the core joined the apple in the boy's stomach. He wiped his mouth on the gray sleeve of his shirt and considered his next step.

The fruit peddlers had packed their wagons and moved off. He searched the market square, picking up a crust of bread here and a bit of a fig there. Still his stomach rumbled. As he stood pondering what to do, he heard a window open above. Before he could move, a stream of slop poured down on the pavement next to him, splashing onto his shoes and stockings. Will cursed at the window. From another window came laughter: "Go on, lad, be on your way before we call a constable after you."

When Will reached the waterfront, he saw water birds scooting across the muddy river bottom, plucking out tiny shellfish left open by the receding tide. On a wharf jutting out into the river lay scraps of fish left behind by a fisherman earlier in the day. Will scurried down, glancing over his shoulder to make sure that no one would try to snatch his dinner away from him. He stuffed the fish scraps into his pocket. They would not make much of a meal, but perhaps tomorrow would be a better day.

By this time night had begun to fall. Oil lanterns outside the taverns flickered to life. Soft light glowed through grimy windows, and muted laughter floated on the evening air. Truth be told, Will was afraid of the dark. He scurried home, trying to ignore the rustling sound of rats coming out to eat. His alley was dark—no oil lanterns lit the night—and smelly. The air stank of tanning chemicals and smoke, rotting food, and human waste. Black soot coated the storefronts; their windows were yellowed with smoke.

Will approached the old cellar under a tanner's house. A broken door covered the entrance to the dirt-floored cubbyhole. He ducked inside leaving the door ajar. The ceiling was so low he had to squat inside. His bed was a mat of straw, and his stove a cast-off bucket. After measuring out a bit of wood and coal from his bin, he saw with disappointment that he had only enough fuel for another day's cooking.

When the fire was lit and glowing brightly, he ran a sharp stick through the fish heads and held them over the flame. He didn't mind waiting for the fish to cook. It was pleasant enough to sit and get warm as he listened to the popping of fat in the fire. When the fish was cooked, Will wolfed it down. Then after watching the last embers burn out, he lay down and fell asleep.

He was in the midst of a dream when the crash of heavy boots awakened him. His door flew open, and a soldier tromped down the stairs into his cellar, torch in hand.

"Get out of bed. We've caught up with you this time."

"Who are you?" Will cried, peering through the darkness at the soldier's black boots on the cellar stairs.

"Get up. We've been looking for you for hours, you rascal."

The next thing Will knew, the soldier was grabbing him from his bed and dragging him up the stairs. The boy stumbled into the street. By the torch's dim light, he saw that he was surrounded by a handful of soldiers.

"I need to go to the bathroom," he croaked.

" Go in the bucket," one sneered.

Will's temper flared. "Lobsterback!" he muttered. "What am I supposed to have done?"

"All innocent now, are we?" He felt a musket butt

press his shoulder. "That won't play with us, lad. We've got witnesses. Besides, a woman—a fruit seller—says you stole a couple of apples from her. It looks like prison for you."

"Liars!" Will spat. "I don't know who you talked to, but they're liars, and you know it."

"Well, they may be liars, but there's a gentleman outside who says you robbed him. Knocked him on the head before taking his purse and horse."

"I never did that."

One of the soldiers slapped him. "Are you so arrogant that you would put your word against the word of a gentleman?"

Will bit his tongue. No good would come from insulting a gentleman. The soldier, seeing that Will was not going to speak, nodded. "You've a bit of sense," he said. "But why did you have to hit him in the face?"

"I never did," Will hissed through clenched teeth. A blow landed on his ear.

"It'll go better for you if you confess to our captain. Do you get my meaning?" Again the soldier slapped the boy's ear. "What's your name, boy?"

"Will Northaway."

"Straighten up, Will Northaway. The captain is here, and he wants to ask you some questions. See that you answer them truthfully."

Will stood shakily. He held his hand to his bloody ear and tried to keep from crying. A short, pear-shaped man with many chins and a powdered wig peered at the boy as though looking at a piece of dung. Then, as Will watched, he took a bit of snuff from a box and placed it gently in his nose. After sneezing twice, he cleared his throat and asked, "Is this the boy?"

"Yessir. His name is Will Northaway. He's the one the peddler complained about."

"Good. A petty thief then?"

"Yessir. No family. No one will miss him."

"Good. Now you go on back to your duties. You'll be well paid for your troubles." He nodded to dismiss his men, who shuffled off in the direction of the river. Before they were out of earshot, the captain added, "I needn't remind you that you did not see Lord Winchester tonight. I wouldn't want to ship any of you off to America."

Will heard a few muffled "no sir's" before the men disappeared down the alley. The captain turned to his aide. "Take Lord Winchester home and don't let him stop anywhere. Deliver him to his servant no matter what he says. Do you understand?"

Feeling dizzy, Will lowered himself to the pavement where he rested his head on the damp stones. A moment later he felt the smooth tip of a boot against his cheek. "Open your eyes and let me see you."

Will's eyes blinked open. Standing over him was the red-faced captain and next to him someone who looked like the captain's dirty cousin. They were nearly the same age, about thirty, but where one was pink and polished, the other was soiled and smelly. His wig was on crooked, and where once three polished silver buttons had hung, now there was one.

The dirty one was having trouble standing. He leaned heavily on the captain and giggled. "Looks like him," he said in a soft, slurred voice. "It's the one. Yes, it's the one."

"That's all then. Get yourself home, William, and don't stop to see anyone. You look frightful and smell worse. Did you close down the gin shop?"

"I was just doing a little wagering at the Dog and Duck."

"I don't care what you do with your money, William. I don't care who you spend time with. But don't come asking me to save your neck anymore. Stay in Westminster, brother. And stay out of trouble. This is the last time. I won't have my career hurt by a drunken brother's weakness for gin and women."

The words rattled around in Will's muddled brain. Somehow he was supposed to take the blame for something Winchester had done. He felt a moment of despair. No one would ever believe him. The captain pulled Will to his feet. "I'm sorry you've gotten mixed up in this," he said. "But you can't go bashing in the heads of gentlemen and stealing their wallets and insulting their ladies. The sheriff won't stand for it."

Will opened his mouth to protest, but the captain gave him a sharp blow to the head. "Listen to me. Everyone in Southwark knows you're a thief. We have a dozen sworn complaints against you. You're going to prison anyway. One more charge does little harm to you, but it does a great deal of good for Winchester."

Still wincing from the blow, Will cried out, "Please don't hurt me. I'll say anything. What am I supposed to have done?"

"That's the attitude, son. You tell the magistrate that you robbed Lord Winchester and hit him and left him lying in the street. You tell him that you never saw a young lady and that you're sure it all happened before midnight. You tell him that, and I'll make sure it goes well with you."

Moments later the horse, with Will mounted behind the captain, cantered down the street, headed to who knows where. The sheriff. Prison. It was all the same. A scrawny boy like Will Northaway would die of disease before he was free. Will suddenly recalled the sign he'd seen that morning. Ye Go, it had said. It was a bitter invitation, for it looked like prison was the only place Will Northaway was going.

Garbage filled the streets between the tannery and London Bridge. Every step the horse took on the uneven pavement jarred the boy's hurting head.

Suddenly a wagon loaded with crates of chickens pulled into the street. Its wooden wheel hit the gutter and snapped off. The captain's horse reared, and Will fell off, landing in the gutter. Chicken crates slid off the cart, breaking open when they hit the ground. The captain struggled mightily to bring his rearing horse under control, but it lunged sideways, throwing the crop-brandishing captain to the pavement. He landed with a thump.

The old farmer stood off to the side of the road, scratching his head as if he didn't know where to start. Should he fix the wheel, gather his chickens, or tend to the red-coated captain, who would be mighty angry when he came to his senses? Will didn't waste a second. He slipped into the shadows, thinking only about how much distance he could put between himself and the gates of Newgate Prison.

TWO

Waking to a rooster's crow, Will stretched against the back of the wagon. It smelled of pigs and chickens, and now that the boy was awake and no longer desperate to hide, he found the odor overpowering. His head ached, and a fire burned in the pit of his stomach. His mouth tasted of blood. He spat and was glad to see that his spit was clear.

In the dawn's half-light Will tried to think. He had to get far enough away that no sheriff or redcoat would ever find him again. He winced as he climbed down from the wagon, gingerly testing his legs and finding them bruised but nothing worse. Even his stomach felt better once he was out of the wagon. He followed the alley past St. Olaves, where he hoped to find a kind curate who would give him a bite to eat. But the church was locked tight.

He wandered through the graveyard where a long hole stood open, waiting to be filled with the corpses of those who couldn't afford proper funerals. Will crossed himself— something he remembered his mother, or was it his Aunt Bridget, doing. They both had died from a fondness for gin. At least that's what he'd been told.

He shook off the memories and kept walking. He had a friend at The George and Blue Bull, less than three blocks away. There he knew he could scrounge something. Will scurried to the rear alleyway where the cooks dumped their garbage and the coachmen parked their rigs.

"Hey, Will," a plump woman called in greeting. "Heard someone was looking for you last night." Then seeing his bruised and bloody face, she added, "Perhaps he found you."

Will froze. "I don't know what you mean, Anna."

"Redcoats asking about a boy named Fish."

Will scowled. "I just came to get something to eat, not to listen to gossip."

"I've some cold beef pie. Cook can't serve it today because the meat was turning. But it's yours if you want it."

Will tried not to appear too eager and followed the woman to the door. She disappeared inside and returned, handing a greasy paper parcel to him.

He grabbed the bundle and stuffed it under his arm. "Thank you," he mumbled. Then, fidgeting awkwardly, he said, "If anyone asks about me, you won't tell him you saw me, will you?"

Anna paused as if deep in thought, and fear began to show in Will's face. Taking pity on the boy, she shook her head. "I've no use for them. Always upsetting everybody. You've nothing to worry about from me."

As Will turned, she grabbed his sleeve. "You should leave this filthy city," she warned. "I don't know what happened to you or why. But next time you may not get away from trouble so easily. If trouble is out to get you, get you it will. That's what my grandmother used to say. Maybe your daddy made a deal with the devil. Your poor mother sure enough did. But I'd run and not look back. Just run and get away, lad."

Before last night the boy would have laughed. He knew how to survive. Will Northaway had never doubted that he could always find a way to eat and drink in Southwark. Why should he risk leaving? But suddenly that certainty was gone. Fear of prison changed everything. For Will Northaway, the risk of staying was suddenly greater than the risk of going.

So instead of laughing, he asked, "And where am I supposed to go? And how am I supposed to get there?"

"America, of course," she said as if he were half-witted. "That's where I'd go if I had any sense. Boston, New York, Philadelphia—they say you can get rich there." She stared into the distance as an idea formed. "You could work for passage. You're a likely strong lad, though you don't look like much. You could apprentice yourself."

"But how would I get to Portsmouth?"

"Now that's easy." She smiled. "I've a very special friend who drives the coach to Portsmouth. Perhaps he'll take you."

Will chewed his thumbnail. "How would I pay him?"

"Have you nothing?"

He shook his head and jiggled his fingers in his pocket as though he might find something in them.

"Anna!" The voice from inside was harsh.

"I'm coming," she yelled and then turned back to look at Will. "I've got to go. Be back here at noon, and we'll see, though I'm making no promises. See that you wash," she added before going inside. "You look and smell disgusting."

Will spent the morning trying to stay out of sight. He didn't dare go far from the inn, for he knew someone was looking for him. When noon came, his stomach was churning—maybe from the beef pie he had forced down but more likely from nerves. The stage, with a single trunk strapped to the top, had arrived and was parked in the alley. The stable boy was unhitching its four weary horses. Will waited until the boy had led the last horse into the stable before venturing to the door. He knocked on the back door and then stood to the side, ready to run for it if the foul-tempered cook answered.

Anna cracked the door open. Seeing Will, she waved

him forward. "My friend, Edwin Flood, said he'd take you along. I told him you were strong and well able to handle a weapon. Have you ever shot a musket?"

The boy shook his head. "Where would I get a gun?"

She shrugged. "Well, he'll do it as a favor for me. Just don't be a bother to him. No whining or complaining, Will."

The boy drew himself up to his full height and tried to ignore the pain in his belly. "Even if I can't shoot, I guess I can use a stick or a stone as well as any man," he said. "I've been fighting my whole life, and though I don't look like much, I'm afraid of no man."

As he talked, a tall man with a weathered face strolled out of the inn. He pinched Anna's arm and laughed when she giggled. Seeing Will and overhearing his last words, the man laughed even louder.

"Is this the protection you've offered me, fair Annie? We'd better not meet any bandits, had we?" He laughed again with a deep belly laugh that shook his whole body.

Will scowled. He knew men like this—rough, hard drinkers, loud. He'd learned to watch them and never trust them. Anna was grinning so broadly that every one of her ten teeth showed. One snaggletooth stuck out over her bottom lip. Stray ends of mousy brown hair peeked out of her starched white cap.

"Women," Will muttered with disgust. And he was one to know. His own mother, so he'd been told by one scullery maid after another, was the silliest of the lot. A bad woman, some of them said, though Will didn't necessarily believe it. Others said she'd been too fond of gin. Liked it better than water. Driven to it by a no-account husband who'd abandoned her with a child.

Will's father—now he was a mystery. Will couldn't remember him, not a bit. Not even a fragment of memory ever came to him. Not like with his ma. Sometimes when he visited Anna, and there was fresh wash on the line, the smell of the cotton drying in the sun would bring his mother painfully close. A whiff of gin as he passed a tavern, a laugh, maybe even the fragrance of a particular soap or perfume would bring back a memory from childhood.

Will had roamed Southwark's streets from one end to the other, trying to waken a memory of his father. He'd ventured over London Bridge. He never missed Our Lady Fair in September. But nothing ever came to him. Not at the fair, not at the gardens, not on the streets. He'd even wandered near the prisons, all five of them, wondering if his pa was inside.

Just then the stage driver interrupted his thoughts. "I'll be leaving on the morrow, lad," he said. "We'll be off at daybreak—no later."

"But I thought you'd be going today." Dismay caused Will's voice to break.

"Well, I've not had my supper now, have I, lad? And I won't have a bit of a boy telling me my business." Already that backslapping, happy-go-lucky, jolly-good-fellow manner had disappeared behind a hard mask. Will knew the look, and he knew he'd better go before the anger turned physical.

He backed away. "Bye, Anna. I guess I won't be seeing you anymore."

She looked at him, her faded blue eyes moist with tears. "You be a good boy over there," she instructed. "Don't let them Yanks mistreat you."

Will raised his hand in a little salute and then turned away. A mysterious lump in his throat made it hard to swallow.

"Don't be mad at your ma," Anna's voice trailed after

him. "It wasn't her fault. If only your pa hadn't gone to America."

Will swung around. "What do you mean?" he demanded. "What do you mean about my pa?" He grabbed her arm.

"Everybody knows that your pa, the no-account, went to America. Said he'd come back when he'd made his fortune. Promised her, and more's the pity, she believed him. Then he went off, and she found herself pregnant—and never a letter, never a note from him. But you knew all of that," she said.

Will was too stunned to speak. Meanwhile, she turned to Edwin Flood, who was leaning on the doorpost, picking at his teeth with the blade of his knife. "I always say, you can't trust men," she said. "But you aren't going to America, are you?" She grinned at him and pushed him toward the door.

"Wait," Will called. The driver scowled, and even Annie, who had a soft heart, looked annoyed with him. But Will pressed on. "I don't even know his name," he whispered. "Where'd he go?"

"Boston, I reckon. Sailed from London. Must have been ten . . . twelve . . . How old are you anyway, Will? Twelve? Well then, it must have been twelve years ago—in '52, I guess." Again she turned to go into the inn, the driver close behind her.

"His name, Anna? What was his name?" Will pleaded.

"Why, his name was Northaway," she said, looking at him oddly. "Just like yours."

THREE

Will left the inn with a new sense of mission. Boston made him think of farms and fresh air, where each man was a landowner or tradesman. Each man was free.

Will wasn't the type of boy to spend much time thinking about freedom. After all, what did freedom mean in Southwark when you were poor and starving, with little chance that life would ever change? He was free, all right, he thought bitterly as he dodged a passing wagon and stepped over piles of dung. Free to starve.

Thinking about leaving Southwark made him look at his city with new eyes, as though seeing it for the first time— or the last. He wanted to fix it in his memory because he knew, just as he knew his name was Will Northaway, that if he left, he'd never see this city again.

He breathed in the bitter, sharp odor of the tanneries. Had he ever known anything else but its stench?

And the noise—was there ever a noisier city? Church and cathedral bells tolled the hours, their high- and low-pitched tones blending with the cries of peddlers selling their goods and the buoy bells tolling.

He wandered into an alley off High Street. A flash of red roused him from his thoughts. He saw, not twenty feet away, one of the redcoats from the night before. At the same moment the redcoat saw Will. He pointed and yelled to a mate, and they set off after the boy.

Will pushed past those who tried to grab him. For every man who tried to stop him, there were two who blocked his pursuers. He led the chase into the market square where he easily slipped out of sight among the throngs of people who crowded the square.

Breathing heavily and feeling every one of the bruises from the redcoats' beating the day before, Will nonetheless felt a surge of glee. Once again he'd escaped! His heart warmed at the thought of the Londoners who had helped him get away. They disliked the bullying soldiers as much as he did now that the end of the Indian wars in America had filled London's streets with redcoats.

He let himself be pushed along by the crowd until he reached the outskirts of the square. Then he broke free and headed toward the river. For the second time he passed St. Olaves, passed the churchyard where he had often slept. More than once he'd stolen a few coppers from its poor box.

The river's aroma—a rich blend of fish, damp wood, and rotting plants—greeted Will before it came into view. He loved this smell as much as he hated the tannery smells. While standing on a rise overlooking the river, he realized that he didn't want to go by stage to Portsmouth. He'd go by sea.

Once he'd made that decision, he looked over the busy river with new interest. This close to London Bridge there were few large ocean-going boats. They moored in the deep water near Rotherhithe. Here many kinds of boats—punts, barges, and fishing boats—floated on the water.

A punt came too close to London Bridge where the swift current running between the arches suddenly grasped it. The little craft rocked dangerously as it was driven toward one stone pier and then another. The punter tried to steer with his poles, but the current took over, pitching the little boat forward. As Will watched, the man's pole flew out of his hand. When he leaned over to grab it, he was thrown into the water. Seconds later the empty punt shot through to the other side of the bridge.

The drama played out so quickly that Will almost believed he had imagined it. But the empty punt, now floating on the calm waters below the bridge, proved otherwise. The boy shivered. How suddenly it had happened. He wondered if the man had family and if anyone would miss him. Then he thought about himself. If he died, was there a soul on earth who would miss Will Northaway?

Will turned his back on the bridge and began the long walk to Rotherhithe. After some time he reached a bend in the river. As he rounded it, the sight of hundreds of ship masts flying flags of many countries greeted him. He watched the flurry of activity around the ships as red- and blue-clad river boys loaded and unloaded cargo and rowed it to the warehouses lining the river.

Will was trying to work up the nerve to approach one of the warehouses when he heard a gruff voice. "You, lad!"

Startled, Will looked up at a tall man who had stopped working and was staring at him.

"Go away. There's nothing for you here. Be off." He had a voice like sandpaper and a face like a piece of carved wood.

"Are you going to Boston?"

"What's it to you?"

"I'm looking to go there. Have you need of a mate?"

"A mate! He asks if we need a mate!" The man bellowed with laughter, inviting the others to join him. "A scrawny, half-dead lad like you? No, we don't need any shark food—and that's what you'd be, dead before you were a week at sea. Now go home to yer mother."

Will's ears burned as he stalked off muttering, "I don't need him or his kind."

Once he was out of sight though, he glanced down at

his clothes. He was a pitiful sight. No wonder the man talked to him that way. His stockings were torn, and his scabby legs showed through the holes. His shirt was ripped at the shoulder, and his face still wore the bit of sticking plaster that Anna had put on his cut. And he hadn't bathed, though Anna had told him to. He spat on his hand and rubbed his cheek, trying to wipe off a bit of the grime that he was sure covered it.

He sat on the wharf and removed his stockings, putting them back on so that the holes were at the backs of his legs. Then he pushed on to the next warehouse, saying to himself, "All they can say is no, and you've heard that word all your life. So get on."

He went from one warehouse to the next without success. Some of the ships had just come in, and they weren't sailing for a while. Others were going to the Caribbean. By late afternoon he was hungry and discouraged and ready to return to Anna's. He'd go to one more warehouse and then head back.

The building was quiet—no barges loaded or unloaded there. He was about ready to turn back, but hunger and desperation pulled him onward. There was a chance, if the door was unlocked, that he would find some food. He found the big doors that faced onto the river open. Inside six lads sat on crates and barrels, smoking pipes and drinking tea. They stared at the newcomer.

"What do you want?" a boy asked lazily after taking a long sip of tea.

"I want to eat," he said.

The boy laughed. He was freckled and red-faced, his sandy hair held back with a thin black ribbon. He looked at his mates and grinned. "Should we share our riches with the poor bloke?" he asked.

"Sure, Tommy, why not?" a dark-haired boy answered. "It's not our stash anyway. And the cap'n won't know."

Tommy threw a hard object at Will. "Have some hard tack," he said with a grin. "Help yourself to a cuppa if you want. I'm Tommy Fenlaw. Who are you?"

"Fi—," Will began to say before correcting himself. "Will Northaway." He walked over to the kettle and poured himself a cup of steaming tea, breathing in its fragrance before turning to face the boys.

"Have a seat." Tommy gestured to one of the barrels.

Will took a bite of the hard tack and winced. The boys laughed. "That's why we drink tea," one said. "Dunk it. It's not bad unless it's wormy. And this is fresh baked. Not more than a month old, I figure."

Will eyed the biscuit suspiciously. He dunked it in his tea, examined it for signs of life, and plopped it in his mouth. Delicious. When he had finished the first biscuit, Tommy tossed him another.

"I wouldn't eat too many in one sitting," the older boy warned. "Especially on an empty stomach. They tend to harden in the gut—feel like rocks if you aren't used to them."

Will soaked the biscuit and popped it in his mouth. Despite the warning, he would have eaten another if it had been offered. But it wasn't.

"You ain't from here," Tommy said in his strange accent. "What brings you to Rotherhithe?"

"I'm looking for passage to Boston, but I'm not having much luck."

"Why Boston? Ain't that where old Cap'n Graham is from?"

"No, he's from Edinburgh. A Scot, he is."

"But he sails from Boston," the first boy insisted, "though he flies the Union Jack."

They all stared out at a three-masted brig anchored mid-stream, the British flag flying from its mast.

"Ah, he wouldn't want to sail with Captain Graham. Don't he make sea sacrifices? Throws a boy overboard at the beginning of every voyage. Came back a boy short last voyage. That's what I heard."

"Don't pay his men neither."

"No, they pay him—with their blood."

"I don't believe a word of it," Will interrupted. "Do you think he'd take on someone like me?"

"You mean someone who don't know his fore from his aft, who don't know hard tack from a rock, and who will be dog-sick for half the trip? He's about the only one who'll take you on. You'll be the likely sacrifice."

Will ignored their laughter. "How do I meet this Captain Graham?" he demanded.

Tommy paused while giving Will a hard once-over. Then with a note of regret, he said, "I'd not bother. He won't like the looks of you."

"What's wrong with my looks?" Will asked, forgetting for a minute how bad he looked.

"He won't like the cuts. Proves you're a brawler, and 'there's no brawlin' on me ship,'" Tommy said, pacing back and forth in imitation of the captain. "He won't like your clothes either. He'll say you're a dirty good-for-nothing and a . . ." Tommy paused, turning to his friends for help.

"Wretched."

"Louse-ridden."

"Mangy."

"Flea-bitten."

"Sounds like you're describing a dog," Will protested with a weak grin.

"He'll think you're a dog," they yelled in unison.

"Well, it matters not at all to me," Will said. "For I'll tell him to consider the potato. It too is dirty, but it sure do satisfy."

"He's made a joke, boys," Tommy laughed. "Problem is, Cap'n don't like to laugh . . . but he does like wit." The sandy-haired lad turned to Will. "Wait for me outside. I'll take you home. If it's possible to clean you up, my ma will do it."

Will had only to wait a few minutes before Tommy joined him. They swung off toward home with Tommy whistling a sea chantey while Will trudged along behind him. Before long they reached a row of brick houses that all looked alike and were joined together. Tommy's stood out because the front porch was swept clean. A pot held a forlorn-looking rose that bloomed bravely despite its grimy surroundings.

"Ma says if that bloomin' rose ever dies, she's gonna die too. So we all do our best to keep it alive." He looked embarrassed as he said it.

"It's a great rose," Will answered. He felt nervous about meeting Tommy's mother. But he followed Tommy through the front door, willing to endure just about anything if it would get him to Boston.

"Tommy's home, Tommy's home." Three little tow-headed boys raced into the room and grabbed their brother by the legs, holding on while he dragged them toward the fireplace. A tiny woman turned from the pot that she was stirring and laughed. "You scags let go of your brother. Dog-tired he is and not needing three little puppies hanging on him. Bring some tea." Though her face was deeply lined, her eyes glittered, and her mouth turned up in a warm smile.

"Ma, this is Will Northaway. He came by the dock asking for a job, and I thought, well, you know . . ." He blushed. "Well, anyway I thought you might help him, you know, clean up a bit."

She gave Will a tired smile. "Fine, fine. Yer pa will be home in a bit, and Robby, and Sarah. You take that tea outside and wash. I don't need the smell of fish to fill the house. Take Will with you and give him the soap. Now go on—be off with you both."

She shooed them out of the tiny house. Tommy pumped water into a basin and handed it to Will along with a bar of soap. "Wash." Will looked at him skeptically. "Go on, wash," Tommy insisted.

"It's not good for me," Will protested.

"I don't know if it's good for you or not, but if you're hungry and wantin' to eat supper tonight, you'd better wash. And do it quick. Me pa will be home and hungry, and he'll be waitin' for no man. And you saw all those little ones. If you aren't at the table, you get no food. So hurry." He hopped back and forth impatiently, waiting for Will to start.

Will handed him the basin and the soap. "You go first," he said, unwilling to admit that he'd never used soap before and wasn't sure how to do it.

Tommy pulled his white shirt off, put the soap in the basin until it was soft and foamy, and proceeded to rub it over his chest and body. Then he stooped by the pump and splashed the cold water on himself until he looked shiny and pink.

Next he handed the basin to Will. "Your turn, and hurry. I think I hear me pa."

Will dabbed the soap on his skin and watched as his body turned from gray to peach. He rubbed a bit harder and saw more streaks appear wherever he scrubbed. The soap smelled a bit like grass, and he sniffed his skin.

"Balsam," Tommy apologized. "Ma likes her soap to smell good, but I don't like smelling like a tree. She sells it in the market. Toffs like it," he added with a touch of pride.

It took Will longer than Tommy because he was so much dirtier. It had been months since he'd been in the river to bathe. Tommy eyed him curiously. "Better wash your hair," he urged. "Ma won't like it if she can't tell what color it is. What color is it anyway?"

"Don't know," Will grunted. "Never looked." He dunked his head under the pump, rubbed it all over with the soap, and rinsed it until it squeaked. When he was done, it stood in spikes all over his head. "Am I done?"

Tommy looked him over. "It'll do. Now let's go eat. I'm starving."

Will stared at the boy. They had just had biscuits and tea. How could he be starving? But Will was not one to turn away food. He followed the other boy back into the house.

Tommy's father sat at the head of the long wooden table. When he saw the boys, he whistled, and what seemed like an army of children traipsed in, taking their seats on the two benches at either side. A bowl of something brown and fragrant steamed at one end of the table. Tommy's mother spooned it into trenchers and set them before the hungry brood.

Will shoveled a spoonful into his mouth, delighting in this unexpected treat. Before he could take another bite, he heard Tommy's father clear his throat. Looking up, he realized that no one else was eating. They were all staring at him. With a jerk he set the spoon down, color racing to his face.

"We'll ask a blessing," Mr. Fenlaw said. As soon as the prayer was done, every hand reached for the bread and began shoveling in the stew. For at least five minutes the room was quiet except for the sound of lips smacking and spoons scraping on wood.

Then as if by signal, the eating stopped. There wasn't a

drop of stew left in the pot. Only gravy remained in the trenchers. Will wondered if it was polite to lick his. He waited and saw that none of the others had lifted the wooden plate to lick it. When no one was looking, he slid his finger into the tasty sauce and stuck it in his mouth.

"So, Will Northaway, you want to go to sea, do you?" asked Mr. Fenlaw.

"Yessir. Anyways I want to go to Boston."

"And what's in Boston for a lad like you?"

Will shrugged. He wasn't about to talk about his father. Besides, Will was suspicious of men. Although Mr. Fenlaw seemed kind, Will didn't trust him—not for a minute. He'd seen too many who became mean and surly after a couple of cups of ale, and he'd bet anything that Tommy's dad was like all the rest.

"Just want to go. I've nothing here, and I've heard stories about jobs . . ." His voice trailed off.

Mr. Fenlaw leaned back in his chair. "Bring me my pipe, Sarah." He stared at Will while he went through the motions of lighting the pipe. Will shifted uncomfortably while the little fellows squirmed. "You may all be excused except for Will and Tommy."

Mrs. Fenlaw took up her knitting by the fire while Sarah cleared the table. The younger boys played quietly on the hearth.

"I can't say that I know Captain Graham well, but I do know his first mate."

Will waited.

"It's not an easy voyage," the older man continued. "And there's no turning back. You can't change your mind. Do you realize that, son?"

"Yessir."

"There's no guarantee that you'll ever see land. The

last boy took sick and never made it back. Buried at sea. His mother never saw him again."

A picture of the man in the punt came to Will's mind, but he pushed it away. "I'm not afraid," he said.

Tommy's father nodded and rose from the table. "Make a place for Will to sleep tonight, Tommy. I'll think about it."

Will would have pestered Mr. Fenlaw, but Tommy pulled him away. "Don't be a fool," he warned. "Let him be. You won't be changing his mind by nagging. Now come on to bed. I've got work tomorrow."

Will followed Tommy upstairs to the room where the boys slept. The little ones were sprawled out on the bed they shared, already asleep. Tommy seemed to fall asleep as soon as he hit the bed, but Will's mind was full of anxious thoughts that kept sleep away. From below he could hear voices and strained to make out the words.

"What will you do?" he heard Mrs. Fenlaw ask.

"I don't know. What do you think of him?"

"I don't see much evidence of a mother's training," she replied.

"You're right. I'd not be surprised if he's running from something. But perhaps he deserves a second chance."

Mrs. Fenlaw said something that Will couldn't catch, and then Tommy's dad said, "John will be willing, I think. Your brother Mattison is as softhearted as you are."

Will smiled. It was a good sign. And this time when he laid his head on the pillow, he had no trouble falling asleep.

FOUR

The brig *Ana Eliza* was anchored midstream among ten other oceangoing vessels. Tommy pointed her out to Will— a black ship whose three masts stood tall against the gray sky, her rigging like hundreds of fine pen marks etched on paper. A Union Jack fluttered from her jib.

She's a fine ship, Will thought. A small barge, flat-bottomed and broad, powered by four rowers, sat ready to push off from the wharf. The craft was piled high with barrels and crates headed for the *Ana Eliza*'s hold. Tommy pushed Will forward. "Hey!" he yelled. "This lad needs a way over. Take him, will you?"

When the men nodded, Will clambered onto the barge, finding a seat amidst the cargo. He gave a halfhearted wave to Tommy, who nodded from the wharf. "It'll be fine, Will Northaway. When you make your fortune, write to me and tell me all about it."

Will squeezed between barrels and crates, being careful to keep out of the way of the oarsmen. He huddled down as it began to rain, feeling the drops soak through his shirt. As the barge reached the side of the ship, he realized how big it was. Even loaded with cargo and sitting low in the water, her sides dwarfed the little barge.

By the time the small vessel was tied to the ship and the cargo transferred, Will was soaked. He looked more like a rescued rat than a seaman. A grizzled sailor wearing a round, flat-brimmed hat, blue breeches, and a blue-and-white checked shirt greeted him. The sailor's hair was pulled back in a ponytail doubled over and stiffened with tar so that it hung like a handle at the back of his neck.

"Are you a river rat, or do you have business on the *Ana Eliza*?" the seaman asked, laughing at his own joke.

"I need to see Mr. Mattison. Mr. Fenlaw sent me," Will replied stiffly. He stood straight, wishing he were a bit broader through the chest and had arms that didn't look so much like elm twigs. Around him lay a tangle of ropes and a pile of musty canvas.

"Where's your trunk? Your ditty bag?"

"I have nothing."

The sailor shrugged and motioned the boy to follow him. The man walked with a funny little hobble, up and down, up and down, swinging his left leg with each step. Despite his awkwardness, he moved quickly, and Will had to hurry to keep up with him—a difficult task when he was worried about falling on his backside on the slick deck.

"Hey, Blue, what's that following you? Must we now bring on boys who aren't yet dry behind the ears?"

Blue laughed, and Will's face burned with embarrassment.

In a minute Blue ducked down a hatch. He led Will to an area in front of the foremast where the crew slept. Hammocks hung in pairs, one on top of the other, all along the sides of the ship. Next to each hammock was a sea chest. A wooden rail kept the boxes from sliding around in rough seas.

A man looked up when the two entered. He stood at least six feet tall and weighed about 200 pounds. It was hard to judge his age, for his skin was like an old piece of leather, brown and lined from the sun. He wore his hair pulled back but not stiffened.

"This boy wanted to see you," Blue announced. "He seems like a fish out of water, slipping all over the deck. And look at the size of him—he can hardly lift a bucket, I reckon—but Mr. Fenlaw sent him."

"Thank you, Blue." While the sailor hobbled away, Mr. Mattison looked Will over.

"How did you get those bruises?"

Will's hand flew to his cheek. "I fell," he said, barely able to get the words past his dry lips.

"Those wounds don't look like they come from a fall."

Will stared back.

"Look, lad, a ship is a small town, a place where we must all trust one another. For weeks on end it's only us in a wide and sometimes brutal sea. We don't have time or patience for liars." He didn't speak unkindly, but his words were direct.

Will blushed as the man watched him. Finally the boy blurted, "Would you take me if I said that soldiers beat me up? Would you? For that's what happened. They grabbed me from my bed and beat me, and I had done nothing, and that's the truth."

The tall man stretched out his legs and considered the boy. "How do you know Mr. Fenlaw?"

The boy pulled from his pocket a sealed letter Fenlaw had given him that morning. "Here," he said. "Mr. Fenlaw told me to give this to you."

As the first mate read the letter, Will looked around the forecastle. The floors were scrubbed clean, and the trunks locked tight. He glanced at Mattison, whose forehead was creased with concentration. Finally the mate turned to the boy, a whisper of a smile on his face.

"Mr. Fenlaw says I should take a chance on you. He thinks well of you, though he knows not why. He's my brother-in-law. Did you know that? No, I guess you wouldn't. And I wouldn't say he is a soft man . . . though he implies that I am." He shrugged, not seeming to mind the insult. "That may be, and yet I won't allow liars on board this ship. So tell me more about these redcoats."

Will took a deep breath while he thought about how much to say. But before he could speak, the man interrupted: "If it won't be the truth, don't bother."

Will had the strange feeling that Mr. Mattison could read his thoughts. It was a new feeling and one he didn't care for, but he didn't dare lie. "They said I had robbed a lord . . . but I didn't . . . I swear. He was drunk and made up a story to cover it up, and he chose me to blame."

"And why you?"

Will hadn't really thought about it before, but the answer was clear. "'Cause who'd care about me? I've got no family. Who'd care if I was in Newgate? People would just think I'd died and good riddance." The words poured forth in a bitter flood.

"So that's how it is. Well, lad, life on board is hard—I'll not fool you. Captain owns this ship. He wants a swift journey, and he wants his cargo to get to Boston without damage. We run a tight ship. No idleness. There are rules on board, and the captain and I enforce them. No questions. You lie, and you'll be whipped. Do you understand?"

Will nodded.

Mr. Mattison rubbed his jaw and stared at the boy, wondering if he was a fool to take on the scrawny, undernourished lad. Finally he said, "I'll take a chance on you. I don't care what you did in London. But if you do it on this ship, you'll answer to me. And I promise you'll prefer the redcoats' justice to mine."

Will nodded again, and Mr. Mattison seemed satisfied.

"Go find Blue," he ordered. "He's the sailor who brought you here. Ask him to get you settled. You can have Joseph's chest and bunk. There are clothes and linens in the chest." Mattison pointed to a hammock and an unlocked chest. "Put on some proper clothes and then go find Blue."

FIVE

When Mr. Mattison left, ducking under the beams as he went, Will opened the trunk. He found a stiff pair of blue breeches and a heavy white shirt. The pants were loose, but there was a length of rope that Will tied around the waist as a belt.

He climbed up on his hammock, testing the way it swung with the ship's movement. When he heard footsteps, he leaped down, but not before Blue saw him.

"A lazy fellow, aren't you?"

"No, sir."

"Well, get up on deck. The second mate is looking for you."

"Yessir," Will answered. "What's his name?"

"Smithson. Mr. Smithson."

"How will I know him?"

"You can't miss him. He'll be the one yelling at the other boy, Jack. Now hurry up."

On deck Will paused for a minute to get his bearings. He looked off toward shore where Tommy's warehouse was barely visible through the fog and rain. The faint outlines of familiar church steeples peeked through the mist. In front of him sailors toiled over huge sails spread out on deck, checking them for tears and rot. Above, sailors climbed the rigging, searching for the frayed rope that could break in a storm. They barely spared him a glance as he wandered by.

"Are you being paid for gawking, is it?" Will turned and faced a young man, not much more than twenty. He was lean and wiry, with a face that was all points and angles—narrow chin, long narrow nose, and eyes set close together.

"I was looking for Smithson," the boy said.

"That's Mr. Smithson," the pointy-faced sailor corrected him. "You call the second mate mister and don't forget it."

"I didn't know—," Will began to apologize.

"There's much you don't know, but that's no excuse. I'm Mr. Smithson. Who are you?"

"Will Northaway," Will said. "I'm the new boy."

"Have mercy on us. It must be Mr. Mattison's doing. What does he care if I have one more skinny runt to make into a sailor?" Smithson cracked his knuckles as he talked. "Never mind," he said. "I've no time for you now. Go find Jack, and he'll show you the ropes."

Will wandered around the deck, trying to stay out of the way of the seamen. When he came around the captain's cabin, he saw another boy, perhaps a year or two older, sitting on the deck, a basket of rope next to him. Will inched closer.

The boy looked up at him and grinned a gap-toothed smile. His face was sunburned, and brown freckles dotted his pug nose. "Have a seat," he said, patting the deck next to him. "You must be the new boy. Everyone's talking about you."

"How can that be?" Will asked. "I just got here."

"A ship's a small place," Jack answered. "We know all about your fight and you being an orphan and all."

Will flinched. "I didn't expect Mr. Mattison to tell everyone," he said stiffly.

"Oh, Mr. Mattison wouldn't say a word. It's Blue who's the talker. A regular town crier. I wouldn't trust him with any family secrets." Jack talked easily. He had a friendly, open face, and Will began to relax.

The younger boy looked at the basket next to him. "What're you doing?"

"Pickin' oakum."

"Oakum?"

"Aye. We pick apart this old rope and use it to fill cracks in the wood. You'll be an expert at pickin' oakum before the voyage is over."

"That don't look too hard," Will said.

"It's not hard, just boring. If Mr. Smithson sees you sitting with nothing to do, he'll scream at you to 'pick some oakum.'"

"What else do we do?" Will asked, grabbing a length of rope out of the basket and picking apart the fibers as Jack was doing.

"Whatever they tell you."

"But who's the boss?" Will inquired.

Jack laughed. "They're all your bosses. Every one of them. It goes like this. Captain owns the boat and is the big boss. Mr. Mattison is the first mate. He's an officer like the captain, and you won't see him going aloft. Mr. Smithson is second mate. He'll work you to death if he gets the chance, but he has to work like an ordinary sailor. You watch, the other sailors don't pay him any mind. Then there are two able seamen, Isaac and Nathaniel."

"Able seamen?"

"Aye, they know how to tie the fancy knots and can go aloft in a storm. That's who I'd want to be with if the ship was going down. And the rest are just seamen. They're okay, though there are some I'd stay away from."

All the while the two picked at the rope until Will's hands were red and raw. He rubbed them against his pants, and Jack said, "You'll build up calluses, but it takes awhile. . . . Take a break, why don't you, until you see Smithson coming."

Will leaned back against a chest. The drizzle had

stopped, and the sun was doing its best to force its way through the ceiling of gray. He let its rays warm his face. The poles were bare. No sails were up, and Will could see six men on the foot ropes under a yard, the wooden cross timber to which the sails were tied. "What're they doing?" he asked.

"Putting up a new sail," Jack replied. "See that man on the end? That's Mr. Smithson."

Will peered up through the rigging and thought he could make out Smithson's face, but he wasn't sure. "How can you tell?" he asked.

"That's easy," Jack answered. "He's doing very little work, and he's doing all the yelling." The boy flashed a grin at Will. "Mr. Smithson is a fine one to get someone else to do his work."

The men aloft moved gracefully across the thin rope that hung below the wooden yard. From below men pulled certain ropes, and the sail above folded like an accordion.

"How do they know which rope to pull?" Will asked because there must have been hundreds of ropes that all looked the same.

"They'd better know," Jack said. "Pull the wrong rope, and you could cut off a man's arm or leg. Pull the wrong rope, and you could throw a man off the yard and to the deck. There's a rule on board—'Know the ropes'—because if you don't, it could be your life."

That night Will slept soundly despite the snores from the other sailors. He woke to bells ringing and Jack, who slept above him, shaking him by the shoulder. "Get up! If you miss breakfast, you'll be starving by lunch. Cook will not save any food for you."

Will rolled out of bed and dragged on his clothes. He was the last one to leave the forecastle and the last one in the galley. Cook filled a metal bowl with something gray and lumpy, and the boy carried it over to the place where Jack sat.

"What is it?" he asked, poking at it with his spoon.

"Cracker hash," Jack answered with a wicked grin. "Go on, try it."

Will looked at the other boy and noticed that his bowl was nearly empty. He dipped his spoon in and raised it to his lips. It was lukewarm and tasted like nothing the boy had ever eaten before. He grimaced, and the other lad laughed.

"He don't like the cracker hash," he said loudly enough for the others to hear.

"I'll eat his."

"What'll Cook say about that?"

"Yea, Cook, the boy don't favor your cooking."

That brought loud laughter from all the men. Cook smiled unpleasantly and wiped his sweaty face on the stained apron that hung from his bulging waist.

Will blushed red and glared at Jack, who only laughed the louder. "If you don't want it, there's plenty who do," he said.

Will took another spoonful and noticed a little gray spot in it. "What's that?"

"Weevil," Jack said. "Don't worry, they're good for you."

But thinking of eating bugs made Will's stomach lurch. "Here," he said, shoving his bowl at Jack. "I'm not hungry."

The older lad smiled and grabbed the bowl, shoveling down its contents before Will could change his mind.

A bell rang, and a cry went out: "One bell and all's well." The men below rose to their feet and made their way out on deck. Will rose to follow, but he was blocked by

Smithson, who grabbed him by the sleeve. The man leaned over until his face was inches from the boy's. When he spoke, a fine wash of spit sprayed over the boy. "We'll be choosing watches now. Pity if you land on mine." And then he was gone.

Will hurried up on deck where he found Jack with the other men waiting for Mr. Mattison. When the first mate came out, the talking stopped, and all eyes turned toward him. He and Smithson took their places, and the boy compared the two. Of course, Mr. Mattison was dressed in a blue suit and powdered wig, and he looked like a gentleman, while Mr. Smithson in his sailor's suit and greased hair looked like a sailor. But there was something that went beyond Mr. Mattison's clothes. Perhaps it was the way the sailors responded to him: Removing their hats. The respectful silence. The way they waited for him to speak.

When the mate did speak, he said simply, "Isaiah for port watch." Isaiah was a solid-looking fellow, barrel-chested and strong, with sharp eyes and long, delicate fingers.

Everyone knew that Mr. Smithson would say, "Nathaniel Peacock," next, for he was the only other able seaman on board. He was a very dark man with a vivid scar across his cheek. When he heard his name called, he spat a stream of tobacco into a small barrel.

The choosing moved back and forth between the two mates as if they were choosing up teams for softball. Wesson, seaman, went to Mr. Smithson; Alfred, seaman, to Mr. Mattison. Finally only Will and Jack remained. Since Mr. Mattison chose first, Will knew he would choose Jack. After all, the older lad was experienced and good-natured. Even Will could tell that. So he was surprised when Mr. Mattison looked at the two with his searching eyes and pointed at Will Northaway.

"My luck," Jack whispered with a shrug. "But Mr. Smithson's not that bad, and I know how to get around him."

"I'm glad it's not me," Will answered. "He doesn't like me a bit."

"He don't like anyone, and not many like him. Just stay out of his way."

Will nodded. It would be easier to stay out of Smithson's way now that they weren't on the same watch.

That night as he lay in bed, Will asked Jack a question that had been bothering him all day.

"Whatever happened to the boy who slept in this bunk?" he asked.

Jack leaned over from the top bunk. This time no smile brightened his face. "He's dead."

Will remembered something Tommy's father had said. "Did Smithson kill him?"

"Of course not," Jack said impatiently. "Would Captain Graham hire a murderer? Joseph took sick with fever and died. That's all."

"Where's his body?"

"Buried at sea. Nothing left but the clothes off his back. The ones you're wearing," he said. "Now go to sleep." The older boy rolled over on his hammock. Before long Will heard his even breathing. But even the gentle slapping of the waves against the hull of the ship couldn't ease Will to sleep. He kept imagining a boy who looked like him slowly sinking beneath the waves.

SIX

Sweet and clean? What does that mean?" Will asked. "Will the captain be smelling our hair to make sure we've washed?"

"Shh," Jack said, nudging him with his elbow. "You could learn something."

They had been summoned like the rest of the crew to the deck where Mr. Mattison and Mr. Smithson stood near an iron anvil. It was the morning of June 4, 1764, and the *Ana Eliza*, having been packed with as much cargo as the handsome ship could carry, was set to leave for the month-long voyage to Boston.

Mr. Smithson bounced on the balls of his feet, jiggling a hammer in his hands and waiting for Mr. Mattison to stop writing in his journal. The second mate, looking pinched and crabby, stared at Mattison with barely concealed impatience. In front of them the sailors, some seated on barrels, others sprawled lazily against the rigging, were laughing and talking or staring quietly across the water. Finally the first mate finished his writing and nodded at Smithson. The second mate pointed at Isaiah and barked, "Are you sweet and clean?"

"Aye."

"Then show me your knife."

Isaiah reached under his shirt and around his back and drew a long knife from its scabbard. He held it out to the second mate with an "I-told-you-so" look, and the second mate nodded.

Will poked Jack. "What was that about?"

"Take a look at the blade," the older boy advised. "The point's been broken off."

Will craned his neck to see, but Isaiah had already put his knife away, and Smithson was calling the next man. "Nathaniel!"

"Sweet and clean," he answered and held out his knife. This time Will could see that the point of the knife was gone, broken clean off, leaving a long sharp blade without a point.

One by one the crewmen came forward when their names were called. Those whose knives were not broken held them out to Smithson, who placed them on the iron anvil and whacked off the sharp point with his hammer, leaving the cutting edge unharmed.

"If I had a knife, I'd not let him do that," Will said.

"You'll be glad the first time one of the men gets mad at you. You haven't been to sea with an angry seaman, but I have. You can't run from 'em. Not like on the street. This old ship's a small place, and if you pour a pint or two of rum down their throats, there's no reasoning with 'em. Captain's just protectin' 'em from themselves."

Will looked around at the sailors, who all looked as harmless as the lame Blue or one-eyed Epp. He snickered at the thought of any of them wielding a deadly knife. "I'm not fooling," Jack said sharply. "You think Epp is harmless because he wears that black patch? I've seen him so drunk that he tried to push a man overboard."

When Will still looked doubtful, Jack hopped to his feet, his own hands balled into fists, ready for a fight. Will glanced around and was relieved that no one was paying any attention to the two of them. He tugged on Jack's pant leg. "Sit down. I don't think you're lying. It just seems funny to me. That's all. Why does Captain hire 'em then?"

"It's the law of the sea. If you're going to be a sailor,

you have to be willing to stick up for your interests—even if it means using a knife."

"Why?"

"I don't know. I figure we aren't like other men. We like adventure. Some are running away—like you, I suppose. And when we've had heavy seas and Cook has burned the biscuits and all the clothes are wet and it's cold and damp, men lose their tempers."

"All I know is, I'd not let anyone ruin my knife," Will said.

Jack scowled. "It ain't ruined. Look at the blade. It can still cut rope and sailcloth. And I'd rather see Epp with a broken knife than have his blade shoved through my belly."

By now all the men had shown their knives to the mates. As the sailors did a last-minute check of the ropes, Will said, "I've not yet seen Captain Graham. When will he come out?"

Just then Jack nudged Will with his foot and pointed toward the captain's cabin where a thin, gray-haired man stood leaning on a cane. His hair was tied back with a simple black ribbon. He was of average height and size, and Will would have taken no note of him except for the pale face that made him look more like a bank clerk than a sea captain.

Tommy had said he was a rich man, but he didn't look rich—not like the London dandies Will remembered. The boy tried to recall what else Tommy and his friends had said about the man—"tight-fisted?" "Mean?" In any case the man wasn't anything like the big, swaggering figure the boy had imagined. Instead, he was like a shadow, gray-skinned, like one recovering after a long illness.

Captain Graham limped to the main mast, staring back at London to the north and Southwark to the south. Gradually the rest of the crew became aware of the captain's presence, and all conversations came to a halt as they waited expectantly for him to speak. A brief smile flitted over his face, but it disappeared as quickly as it had come. He began to talk in a voice so low that Will had to lean forward to catch his words before they were carried away by the breeze.

"Men, we are setting out on a long journey. Though we have made this crossing many times, we still need God's blessing. Work hard, obey orders, and we can trust God to deliver us safely."

It was a short speech, and when it was finished, the men shook hands with the captain and Mr. Mattison. Captain Graham seemed almost embarrassed by their attention. He nodded absentmindedly at Will and Jack before limping off to his cabin.

Will stared at the retreating figure before being called back to the present by the activity around him. The ship's bell rang out a sweet, pure sound. Men scurried aloft, climbing as sure-footedly as monkeys up the rigging. On deck sailors tightened some ropes and loosened others. Above them the huge canvas sails opened and fluttered and filled with air, while below the anchor rose from the depths where it had been holding the ship in place. Freed from its anchor and powered by the wind, the *Ana Eliza* broke the bonds holding it to England and began its long voyage to the New World. Behind it the hulls of the ships still moored in the river faded away, their masts becoming faint lines on the horizon.

Will stood and watched, not sure how to explain the knot in his stomach and the lump in his throat. He felt a hand on his shoulder and turned to find Mr. Mattison standing behind him. "It's an awesome sight, lad. Never fails to impress me. How quietly the old sails do their work."

It was just so. There was no grinding or groaning to

reveal how hard the sails worked to push the ship along the Thames, past the London skyline and miles of farmland as the mighty river cut its way through England on its way to the North Sea.

"Will you miss this old land?" Mr. Mattison asked, seeming in no hurry to put the boy to work.

Will shrugged. "It's the only home I've ever known, sir. But it ain't been that friendly to me."

"No, it hasn't been. Perhaps things will go better for you in Boston. Perhaps they will. Now go on and rest. We've three and a half hours before duty."

Most of the men on Will's watch went down to the forecastle to catch some sleep, for many had stayed on shore late the night before. Others played cards. But Will had no desire to sleep. He strolled the deck, observing the men of the starboard watch as they moved from mast to rigging, checking ropes and knots. The heavily loaded ship rode deep in the water, shrugging off the small waves that splashed up against its hull.

Already the men aloft were singing. Will couldn't make out the words, but they seemed to catch the rhythm of the ship. He watched with admiration as the seamen walked sure-footedly on the yards. Epp caught the boy's admiring glance. "Are you wanting to join us?" he shouted. "Come on up—the view is fine and the winds light." The words sounded playful, but Will knew it was a taunt.

Just then Jack came up behind him, carrying a bucket. "It's harder than it looks," he warned. "There's a lot of wind up there even though you can't feel it on deck."

Will looked up and could see it was true. The sails were full, but on deck there was but the slightest breeze. Just then Mr. Smithson came into view. He stopped in front of the boy, regarding him through hostile eyes. "Are you on starboard watch, boy?"

Will started to scowl but thought better of it. "No sir. Port watch, sir."

"Then go down and get your rest. Your duty will come soon enough."

Will had dozed off. The cry from the watch policeman, "Seven bells and all's well," roused him from his slumber. He jumped from his hammock, dragged on his clothes, and ran to the galley. Despite his hurry he found himself at the back of the line because every seaman who came in after him pushed the boy aside and crowded in front of him. Will rocked impatiently from foot to foot, holding his metal plate in his hand, hoping the food would be good and that there would be enough for him.

When it was finally his turn, he looked with disappointment at the small bit of stew and biscuit that Cook had given him. But it didn't matter. No sooner had he sat down to eat than the cry went out, "Eight bells and all's well." The seamen shoveled down the last bits of food and ran out on deck. Will lingered, trying to finish his lunch, but the meat was tough, and he had to chew and chew each piece. He was still sitting when Mr. Smithson and the sailors from the first watch pushed through the door.

Smithson glared at the boy. "I heard eight bells. Get out there with your watch."

Will pointed at his plate, but Smithson shook his head. "Do you think I care about your tender belly? I warned you about shirking. Now get out there." Without waiting for Will to rise, the mate grabbed the boy's plate and dumped his food on the floor. Cook, seeing the mess but not how it came to be there, cursed loudly and boxed the boy on the ears, sending him running out of the galley and up to the deck.

Mr. Mattison was waiting for him. He shoved a broom into the boy's hand and ordered him to work. By now Will's temper had the better of him. "I didn't figure I'd be doing housework," he grumbled, quietly enough so that Mr. Mattison did not hear but loudly enough for Alfred, who was standing next to him, to hear.

"Well, matey, so swabbing decks is not for you? Let's see you draw the water. Go on, Goose, let the boy draw the water."

Will felt he had gotten off to a bad start. He staggered over to the side of the ship where Goose held a canvas bucket tied to the end of a rope. He was a baldheaded man with a long neck covered with tiny bumps that looked like the skin of a plucked bird. Goose handed the large bucket to the boy and then stood back, his well-muscled arms folded against his chest, a sly grin on his bronze face.

Will looked at the bucket and forced a smile. What did they take him for—a fool? It was lighter than the iron pots in Southwark, and he'd lifted them plenty of times. He nonchalantly threw the rope and bucket over the side and watched as the canvas bag dropped into the water. It caught and tipped and began to fill. Within moments it had sunk beneath the surface, and the boy, who had been only half minding what was going on, felt the rope pulling through his hands. Without thinking he tightened his grip, and the rough fibers tore at his tender palms.

He looked up at the circle of seamen whose hard and unyielding faces formed a wall around him. Turning his back to them, he bent over the rope and pulled with all his might, but the rope barely moved, and the bucket stayed under the water. He pulled again but without success.

Before long his hands were raw, and his upper arms trembled with the effort.

"Why, the last boy could lift a bucket single-handedly," someone said.

"Sure he could. I remember the time he swabbed the deck in less than an hour, and even Mr. Mattison could find no fault."

"That's right. A fine boy he was. We'll never find one to match him—and surely not in this puny lad we have here. Ashamed I would be if he were my son."

The taunts went on until Mr. Mattison, hearing the raised voices, strolled over from the helm where he had been taking measurements for the ship's log.

"I see no work getting done here," he said sternly. "Get on with it. A watch is little enough time to do all that needs doing, but if you feel the burden of too much free time, I can fix that."

"I'll show the boy how it's done," Alfred said with a sigh as the mate walked away. Rough hands pushed the boy aside and grabbed the rope.

In rhythm Alfred and Goose looped the rope over the spar, providing leverage for the heavy bucket. They sang a pulling song, "Heave ho, heave ho," in rhythm with their work, and soon they had hauled up the bucket and dumped the water into a large wooden trough. They repeated the task until the trough was filled, and sweat dripped from their brows. When there was enough water, Epp, the little sailor with the eye patch, took a smaller bucket, filled it with water, and dumped it in front of Will and a silent sailor named Jakob.

Jakob grabbed his broom and began to sweep the water back and forth across the deck. Will joined in, and together they moved along the left side of the ship.

One bell, two bells, five bells, six—Will hardly noticed as the time passed. His arms and back ached, and his mouth was dry. Next to him Jakob worked steadily. Although Will tried to talk to him, the white-haired fellow merely grunted in response.

As soon as the helmsman called out, "Eight bells," Will put up his broom and ran for the galley. He was dog-tired and hungry and thirsty, but a hand collared him at the galley door and jerked him back.

"Where are you headed?" Epp demanded.

"To eat," Will replied.

"A glutton you must be. It's not your hour to eat. You've got nearly two hours to wait."

Will groaned. If it had been anyone else but Epp, he would have begged a bit of food. But there was something sly and unpleasant about the one-eyed sailor, and Will would not let him see how miserable he was. He went down to the forecastle and sat on his hammock, looking at his raw, red hands. The other men paid no attention to him, and he had too much pride to ask for help. He tore strips of cloth from his old shirt and wrapped them around his hands. Although the shirt was grimy, at least the boy could bind the blisters and give them a chance to heal.

He made sure that he was first in line when the call came for dinner. Cook had recovered from his earlier anger and, perhaps because he felt guilty for hitting the boy, filled his plate before the rest of the crew came pouring in. The boy shoveled the food down, hoping to have time for seconds. But before he could ask for more, the bells rang, and the cry went out: "Four bells, and all's well."

"All's well but my belly," he groaned. He dragged up on deck and bumped into Alfred.

"Look lively, boy," the sailor barked.

Will muttered an apology and backed away, meaning to get as far away from the sharp-tongued Alfred as he could. But he hadn't gone more than a few feet when another sailor called to him to fetch a rope. And then another wanted a needle. And another, some lamp oil. And Mr. Mattison, a fresh quill. For two hours the boy ran back and forth, fetching this and that, until the welcome sound of the bells rang out. By watch end the ship was ready for the night, and Will was ready for sleep.

SEVEN

It took days to navigate the Thames and the English Channel, and Will came to expect to see the coast on the starboard side. But one morning when he woke from his sleep and went on deck, he looked out and saw only water. Sometime during the night the *Ana Eliza* had slipped into the open sea.

He looked up at the sails that rose in splendor above him. It was an awesome sight. The *Ana Eliza* seemed such a tiny thing bobbing on the waves. As the fair skies and calm waters gave way to dirty weather, Will began to feel a bit of anxiety. The wind picked up, and the swells grew. Mr. Mattison ordered some sails furled and braced.

At seven bells Will staggered to the helm. "You're looking a bit green, lad," Isaiah said. "If you feel sick, heave in a bucket or in the head," meaning the bathroom. "Or over the side."

Will looked at him blankly and then lurched to the side of the ship and emptied his stomach into the sea.

"It hits even the best of them," the well-muscled sailor said kindly, for which Will was grateful. "You'll not want breakfast."

"But I'm hungry, sir," the boy said, remembering the hunger pains he had been feeling not too long before.

"No, I don't think so," Isaiah laughed. "You may have been hungry, but now you're sick. At watch end, go to bed."

Will would have protested, but a wave of nausea swept over him and sent him back to the side of the ship. As long as he leaned over the side, the cold spray and brisk air brought relief, but when he tried to stand, his legs were like rubber. He lost his balance and found himself lying helplessly on the deck. Isaiah carried him to the forecastle and put him to bed where he lay groaning in misery.

That's where Epp found him a little later. A kind man would have let Will sleep, but the sailor said in a loud voice, "I need some water, boy. Fetch me some fresh water." When the boy didn't answer, the sailor pulled the thin blanket off Will's shoulders. "Mebbe you didn't hear me. I said, fetch me some water."

Will dragged himself to a sitting position as another wave of nausea swept over him. "Why not Jack?" he groaned.

"I'm asking you."

Will licked his parched lips and rose on shaky legs. He staggered to the galley where he filled a mug from the barrel of fresh water.

When he returned, Epp grabbed the mug and sniffed its contents. "This ain't grog," he said, referring to the mixture of rum and water the crew usually drank. "You've no more sense than a fool." He threw the water on the floor.

Will fell back on the bed, not really caring what else the sailor might say.

The bells rang, forcing Epp to go. "I must go, but I'll be back. I'm not finished with you."

The hours dragged on. Will's stomach heaved, and the bucket beside his bunk saved him more than once. When he finally awoke, the forecastle was quiet, and his blanket hung off his hammock as though he had wrestled with it. A cloth lay on the floor, but the foul bucket had been emptied, and a mug of sweet tea sat in its place. Tears filled Will's eyes at the simple, kind gesture. He eased himself to a sitting position and took a sip of tea. The sweet liquid warmed his stomach.

The first thing Will saw when he went on deck was a broad blue sky stretching across the heavens in all directions and melting so effortlessly into the sea that it was impossible to tell where sky ended and sea began. A gentle breeze touched his face, and he stood for a moment basking in the sun's warmth like a turtle on a rock.

Mr. Mattison stood with the big log book in hand. The mate glanced up and gestured to the boy. "Feeling better, son?"

Will nodded, embarrassed.

"There's no reason to be ashamed," the mate said. "There's not one of us who wasn't sick the first time we took to sea. Not one. And don't let the men tell you otherwise. You're still looking a bit off, but a bite to eat and some hot tea should put you to rights. It's nearly eight bells. Go on down to the galley and ask Cook to get you some tea with lots of molasses."

The first mate's unexpected kindness made the boy smile. "Shall I rest a bit longer, sir?" he asked, putting on a long face.

Mattison grinned back. "We aren't running a hospital ship. Once you have your tea, lad, come back on deck. You're on duty, and there's work to be done."

Will worked hard throughout the week, but he looked forward to Sundays. Sunday was the Sabbath, and on sea, as on land, the Sabbath was a day of rest. Captain Graham always read from the Bible and prayed. A few sailors remained on watch, and the mate kept up his logbook, but aside from the essentials, the sailors were free to do laundry, spin yarns, fish, and rest.

Sunday was about the only day that Will spent much

time with Jack. At first Will sought him out, for the older boy was a good teacher. But it wasn't long before Will began to dislike his instruction. The older boy was quick with a joke, most of them played on Will. The other sailors thought it great fun to see the new boy tripping over ropes or getting tied into his bed sheets, but Will hated it.

While Jack's humor was not intended to be mean, Epp seemed to delight in tormenting Will. He was sharp-tongued and a good mimic. He mocked the way the boy talked and walked, performing his act behind the boy's back and ending it with an account of the last boy's death. "Your time is nigh," he'd say in a solemn voice. "I feel the threat of death all around you."

Will laughed along with the others, but secretly he hated the jokes. He found himself superstitiously avoiding all the things Epp teased about. Several times he lost his temper, but that only made the sailor laugh, pleased to have drawn blood.

"Ignore him," Blue advised. "It's just Epp." But Will found his advice hard to take.

Will had learned the ship's routine, sleeping in four-hour stretches and eating quickly before the food could be taken from him. He knew how to trim lantern wicks and scrub brass, to holystone the deck (rub it with a rough stone) in wet weather and drop a line over the side for fish on calm days. He even grew a sailor's stomach, shoveling down the "salt horse" as if it were fresh meat and lapping up a bowl of cracker hash without flinching at the occasional weevil. He knew by heart Mr. Mattison's favorite saying: "The devil soon finds mischief for idle hands to do."

One day during the second week at sea, Will was on duty when Epp cried out, "Sail ho!" All hands looked to the starboard side where a two-masted brig was sailing from the west.

Will's excitement mounted. For weeks he had longed for the sight of another ship. Its prow was a knife cutting through the smooth ocean, its sails a magnificent sight. "How beautiful!"

"That's nothing. I'll be captain of an even bigger ship," Jack bragged.

"Oh, go on," Will responded with annoyance. "You're a boy like me. If you'll be a captain, then I'll be the king." He turned his back on the older boy and focused his attention on the other ship, which was drawing near enough for Will to read the name on its black hull. "*The Britannia.*"

"It's true, you know," Jack insisted. "I'm only a boy because my father insists that I work my way up."

"Oh, sure, and my uncle owns the whole British fleet, he does. That ship there is mine, and any other ship we might see flying the Union Jack," Will snorted.

At that moment Wesson approached the boys. "Jack, take yourself off and see if you're needed by the captain," he ordered.

Will looked up, surprised to see the burly sailor squatting down in Jack's place, his cheek full of tobacco. He spat onto the deck and then wiped his mouth with the back of his hand.

"I've been wanting to talk to you, lad, but you seem to keep to yourself. I've seen how Epp bothers you. Ignore him, for he means no harm." The thick-necked sailor spat again as they watched the ship draw near. "It can be hard to know who to trust," he added.

Again Will shrugged, but Wesson wouldn't let it go. He pointed at Jack's retreating figure and said, "He's a good lad, easy to have on board."

"Not so easy if you're the butt of his jokes," Will said.

"Thin-skinned, are you? Surely your pa told you to

toughen up." The sailor absentmindedly picked some oakum as he stared off to sea.

"I'm plenty tough," Will said.

"P'raps in some ways, but not in others. Tell me, why are you going to Boston?"

"To find my father," Will said, flicking the little bits of rope into the air and watching the wind carry them away.

"Your father lives there?"

"Yes. . . . He's a great merchant," he added, looking sideways at Wesson. The lie had slipped out without thought.

"A merchant?"

Will nodded solemnly. "Yessir. He sent for me. Going to take me into the business, he is." Once Will started on this path, the lies became easier to tell. All the stories he had told himself were ripe for telling.

"If he's so wealthy, why did you show up on this ship dressed in rags?" Wesson's face showed that he didn't believe the boy.

Will looked over at the captain who was leaning on the rail, talking through his brass speaking trumpet to the captain of the other ship. Sailors lounged on deck, waiting for the captain or first mate to call them back to duty. "My father wanted me to learn to get by on my own," he said. "He made a deal with my mother: If I could survive on the streets of London by my wits for a year, then I should come to Boston and join him. So here I am."

Wesson shook his head doubtfully. "That's quite a tale," he said standing up. "You're either a fine liar or a fortunate young man."

Will shrugged. Wesson could never prove he was lying, he told himself. Still he felt a twinge of nervousness. What if Wesson blabbed the story all over the ship, and it came to Mattison's attention. "I think I'll go listen for news," he said.

Wesson watched the boy dart away, a calculating expression on his face.

The next several days Wesson seemed to pop up every time the boy had a moment to himself. Will thought his behavior strange, for it meant that he often left his watch to talk to the boy. Sometimes the sailor offered him extra bits of food or offered to do favors for him, especially when Jack was nearby. Soon even Jack had noticed the sailor's behavior. "Why is Wesson being so nice to you? It ain't natural."

Will found himself defending the sailor despite his own doubts. Besides, he liked having a friend. It was nice to get extra food. But more than that, he enjoyed the sailor's attention. Wesson was funny and had an endless supply of stories, which he loved to tell. Sometimes, especially when Will was on watch during the night, Wesson would sit with him on deck and encourage the boy to tell stories about his father.

Will liked those times. The more he talked about his father, the more real he became. Will could picture him and hear his voice. He painted pictures in his mind of his house in Boston and the servants he employed. Giving voice to those pictures brought them to life.

For a week the boy basked in the pleasure of his new-found friendship. But then a strange thing happened. He was picking oakum on deck when he heard a bellow from below and saw Wesson barreling toward him, his jaw working furiously as he shouted Will's name.

The boy stepped backwards as the angry seaman grabbed him by the shirt, lifting him several inches off the ground. "Where is it?"

"What?" the boy sputtered. "What are you talking about?" He licked his lips nervously.

"You know what. The knife. Where's my knife?"

Will stared dumbly at the sailor. "Shh!" he pleaded. "Stop screaming, or someone will hear you."

"I want someone to hear me, you thievin' brat. I'm kind to you, take you under my wing, and this is the thanks I get."

"But I didn't do anything," the boy pleaded. "Please. Tell me what you want, but stop screamin.'"

Wesson released the boy and lowered his voice. "I'm talking about my ivory-handled knife. The one I showed you the other day. The one you admired so much."

Will nodded. Wesson had spent an hour teaching him the basics of carving.

"Well, it's missing, and I think you took it."

"But why me?" the boy asked. "I don't have it. Search my trunk if you want."

"I'll do that. I promise you, if I find it there, I'll tell the captain—and you'll be whipped or thrown in the brig."

Will felt sweat drip down his back and armpits. "Let's go look," he said, eager to prove his innocence. Wesson stomped off, dragging the boy along in his wake. The sailor jerked open the lid of Will's trunk and poked his hand around in it. It only took a second before he faced the boy, a smirk on his face. In his hand he held the knife.

"What do you say now, boy?"

Will swallowed. "I don't know how it got there. I didn't do it. I promise."

Wesson pressed the blade against the boy's cheek. "We're going to talk."

Will nodded, looking around at the sleeping figures on their bunks. "On deck," he said.

This time Will led the way, and Wesson followed closely on his heels as though he feared the boy would escape. When they reached the rear mast, the sailor reached out a hand

and grabbed him. "You're in big trouble now, lad. If I go to the captain, you'll be whipped and held for jail."

Will knew that no one would believe him, especially not Mr. Mattison, who knew the story of the redcoats.

The sailor was in no hurry. He felt the boy's nervousness and pressed the knife a bit harder against his cheek. He said in an oily voice, "Perhaps we can work out a private understanding. Your father is a wealthy man. Surely he'd want to save his only son—you are your father's only son, aren't you?" Wesson paused. "It would be a simple thing for you to tell your father that you have certain debts that you are honor bound to pay. Once I'm paid—100 pounds sterling should do—I promise to forget this matter."

Will's heart was beating so hard he was sure the sailor could hear it. A bitter smile crossed his face as he imagined asking his imaginary father to pay his debts. He started to tell Wesson the truth about his father, but the hard look in the seaman's dark eyes stopped him. How could it hurt to carry the lie a bit further?

"All right."

The sailor grinned smugly as though particularly pleased with himself. Will gave the sailor a puzzled look, and then it struck him. Wesson had put the knife in Will's trunk. The thought made him furious. "You know I didn't take your knife," he said, flailing at the big sailor.

Wesson grabbed the boy's wrist in his beefy hand. "My word against yours," he smirked. "Who do you think the captain would believe?"

"You won't get away with this!"

"Laddie, who'll stop me? I've been sailing for years, and I've barely two coins to rub together. This is my chance, and I'd be a fool not to take it."

The absurdity of the situation struck the boy, and he

began to laugh. Wesson looked at him as though he'd gone crazy. "Shh, you'll wake the watch."

"What do I care?" the boy gasped.

Wesson struggled to regain control of the situation. "You'll force me to tell the captain," he threatened.

Will looked with hate at the sailor. He feared that Mr. Mattison would hear of his lies. He still remembered the first mate's warning. So he stilled himself, shaking off the sailor's hand. "You win," he said.

Wesson nodded. "I'll collect when we get to Boston. Don't think you can put me off." As he moved away, he ran the knife blade softly down the boy's cheek, drawing blood. "That's so you don't forget our deal," he said in the boy's ear. "See that you remember it."

EIGHT

The next several days were quiet enough. The cut was not deep, but it left a red scar from Will's cheekbone to his chin. He made up a story about cutting himself on a piece of wire, which no one really believed, but which they seemed happy to accept in order to avoid trouble.

Wesson still hung around, but now Will did his best to avoid him. Jack noticed the boy's anger with the sailor. "What's up with Wesson?" he asked.

"Nothing."

"I don't believe you," Jack said. "You look like you could kill him. Something happened, and maybe I'll find out."

"Just mind your own business."

Some days later Will was in the forecastle when he saw something glittering on Wesson's hammock. He cast a quick glance over his shoulder, and when he saw that no one was around, he crept closer, half expecting the seaman to pop out and scare him. A grin crossed his face when he realized what he'd found: Wesson's knife. The very knife he'd been accused of stealing. He looked around again, and then without much thought he stuffed the knife in his pocket. It would serve the sailor right.

Once the deed was done, Will was eager to get rid of it. He had no intention of stealing the knife. He just wanted Wesson to miss it. So he ran on deck, dropping it into the first basket he came upon. He had just rid himself of it when Mr. Mattison called to him. "I want to show you how to measure our speed. There's a fair wind, and we'll make good time today."

The next hour was one of the hardest the boy had ever spent. Mr. Mattison began patiently explaining how important accurate measures were if the ship was ever going to find its way to Boston. But although Will tried to listen, he kept expecting Wesson to discover the missing knife. More than once the mate scolded him for inattention.

When it was time to take the measure, he was given a thirty-second sand glass and told that at a certain point he was to turn it over and then yell "Stop" when the sand had run out. It was a simple task, and ordinarily the boy could have handled it without difficulty. But it was no ordinary day, and time and time again he forgot to turn the timer until all the knotted rope had already played out. Or he forgot to shout "Stop," and they had to begin again. Blue, who was holding the reel of rope over his head, and Epp, who was throwing the lead-weighted log chip into the water, both yelled at him.

"Mr. Mattison, the boy hasn't the brains for this job. Let him go back to painting, and let us get on with it."

"He's slow-witted—it's a fact."

"Or maybe daft or deaf."

"I always knew he was thick. . . . Thick as a door."

"Come on, Mr. Mattison. Have pity on us. We've been trying for dead reckoning for an hour. Enough."

Finally the boy's inattention was too much for even Mr. Mattison. "I don't know what has come over you," he said. "But see that it doesn't happen again. Go and find Isaac, and have him put you to work with a brush."

Wesson realized he had lost his knife later that same day when Smithson asked him to repair a sail. Pleased with his ship's progress, Captain Graham had made a rare appearance on deck. He ordered a double ration of rum all around and then circled the deck with Mr. Mattison. Will saw Wesson drink several glasses before going down to fetch his knife. The boy slipped away, sure that the sailor would come looking for him. But it wasn't until sundown that Wesson found him. He stared at the boy through sun-reddened and liquor-blurred eyes. Then he grabbed him by the shirt and leaned close so that Will could smell his rummy breath. "Where is it?" he slurred, spraying spit on the boy.

Will tried to pull away, but Wesson had a strong grip and held on tight. "Get away from me," the boy hissed through clenched teeth.

The sailor leaned heavily against Will as though they were dancing partners. "My knife," he slurred. "Where's my knife?"

"I don't have it," Will muttered.

"Shut up," Wesson snarled, trying unsuccessfully to box the boy on the ear. Just then Mr. Smithson walked by. "What's going on here?" he barked.

Wesson loosened his grip but did not let go altogether. He peered blearily at the second mate and then back at Will, who had taken on an air of wide-eyed innocence.

The boy was the first to speak. "He grabbed me," he said. "He's drunk and babbling nonsense about his knife. P'raps he dropped it overboard."

The sharp-faced second mate looked at the boy suspiciously. "Most likely you've done something to provoke him," he said, looking at his seaman with disgust. "Only he's too drunk to tell me about it."

Wesson hiccupped and leaned toward the second mate.

"Get away from me," Smithson roared. "I'd say you had more than double rations." He turned to Will, his pointy face drawn tight. "If I find you've had anything to do with this, I'll make you pay."

The next Sunday found Wesson still stewing because he hadn't found his knife. He stalked around the forecastle where some of the men were resting, accusing Will to anyone who would listen.

"It was the boy. He took my knife."

"You were drunk," Blue said wearily after hearing the complaint for the tenth time. "You probably dropped it somewhere. Leave the boy alone."

Wesson scowled at the lame sailor and moved on, looking for someone who would listen. He hadn't gone more than a few feet when the lookout's whistle blew three times.

"All hands! All hands!" Sailors hustled to their feet, pulling on clothes and oilskins and shoving their feet into their boots. They poured out on deck. In the distance lightning flashed, and dark, billowing clouds gathered overhead.

"It's dirty weather," Blue shouted into the wind. "You'll earn your sailor's stripes today." The wind picked up, and the boat began to pitch, carried aloft on the swells. Men, some just roused from their sleep, scurried up the tarred ratlines, careful to keep on the weather side of them so they wouldn't be blown off.

"What're they doing?" Will shouted to Jack, who was busy closing hatches and tying down loose barrels.

"Furling the sails," the older boy yelled over the wind. In the distance a huge bolt of lightning flashed across the sky, and about six seconds later the boys heard the sound of thunder. Men on deck pulled ropes, and the huge sails crumpled into loose folds of fabric.

"Storm's still about three miles away," Jack said. "P'raps we'll avoid it altogether."

"Then why not wait to take down the sails?" Will yelled.

"Are you a fool? Once these sails get soaked, they're heavier than the anchor. It makes the work twice as hard, and it's hard enough as it is. They could snap a mast like a twig."

For the next several minutes, sailors dashed about in a frenzy from one crisis to another. Suddenly, the storm was upon them, unleashing its full fury on the ship, knocking it about like a toy in the paws of a kitten. With three sails still catching wind, the men on deck grew more anxious.

"Is everyone aloft who's fit to go aloft?" the mate shouted.

"Aye, sir," roared the helmsman, who had lashed himself to the wheel.

"I'm going up!"

Will turned and saw Wesson beginning to climb up the ratline. The ropes sagged under his weight.

"What's taking them so long to furl those sails?" Mr. Mattison cried. By now heavy rains drenched the decks. The seas were like mountains, and water washed over the sides of the ship. Anything that wasn't nailed down was swept over the ship's side.

Will clung to a railing, his face white, and his thoughts grim. "Shouldn't we go below?" he asked.

"You can't," Jack yelled. "If the ship goes over, those inside will drown. At least on deck we have a chance. Grab a rope and lash yourself tight."

The middle mast creaked and shuddered. Will's stomach churned. He let go with one hand and reached for the tail end of a rope, wrapping it around his waist and the rail before tying it off. Even with the rope, he clung to the rail with all his strength, gripping until his hands hurt.

Clouds had blotted out the sun. Rain like razors sliced

through the air. Still two sails caught wind despite the efforts of the men to bring them down. The main mast swayed and twisted as the winds caught and then loosed the sails. Up above in the rigging seamen, as small as toy soldiers, struggled, hidden in darkness except when lit up by lightning.

Finally all but one sail had been furled. A few of the seamen made their way, inch by inch, down the rigging. The rest stayed aloft, fighting the wind and the wet canvas to bring the last sail under control. From below, Will and Jack watched them wrestle the sail and begin their long, dangerous descent down the ratlines. Their progress was agonizingly slow, for the wind had begun swirling like a whirlwind. A flash of lightning revealed a lone figure moving jerkily along the top yard.

"What's wrong with him?" Will yelled at Blue, pointing at the struggling man.

Blue shielded his eyes and peered up through the biting rain, which ran down the creases in his face. "Looks like he's using only one hand," the old seaman said. "Fool."

The sailor moved clumsily down the rigging and had come about halfway when the wind shifted. Suddenly it was blowing at him, pushing him away from the ropes he clung to. Will could see him grabbing for the ratlines, holding his body against the thin ropes that stood between him and death.

The next few moments were full of confusion. One by one exhausted sailors descended the ratlines and lashed themselves to the railings. By the time Will looked up again, the sailor was gone. The boy sighed with relief. He must have made it down.

The storm battered the ship for ten minutes more. Then, as suddenly as it had appeared, it was gone, leaving only rain behind. It had lasted no more than an hour, but in that time the ship had taken a beating. Will watched the captain, whom he had seen quietly giving orders throughout the storm, take a slow walk around his damaged ship. Several of the sails were torn, and the ship had taken on water, but the *Ana Eliza* had survived.

Later that evening, when the sea had settled and the rain ceased, the captain again came out. Cook measured out grog to the sailors, who huddled together wearily. "God spared us that time," the captain said. "So let us toast his goodness and mercy."

"Aye. Praise God," they said, staring across the vast sea, which stretched before them like a piece of blue cloth.

For an hour they sat, spinning tales of other storms and close calls. The grog warmed them, and the gently rocking ship comforted them. Suddenly Epp looked up from his cup and asked, "Where's Wesson? I've not seen the bloke. He'd not like to miss this bit of drink."

"I've not seen him either," Blue said.

Jack hopped up. "Maybe he's in the head or down below."

"Stop jawing about it and go look," Blue snapped.

Jack returned minutes later with a puzzled expression. "He's not about. I looked everywhere."

Isaiah stood up and pushed the boy. "Of all the lazy lads. You weren't gone long enough to look everywhere. Now the two of you boys go on and find that good-for-nothing sailor."

Will joined Jack, and together they searched the ship. Even when it became clear that Wesson was nowhere on board, they hesitated to return and make a report.

"You go," Jack urged.

"No, you go," Will answered. "I've not seen him since he went aloft."

"Went aloft? Wesson rarely goes aloft. He's too heavy. Swings about like a fat ape up there."

"Well, I saw him go up," Will insisted.

Mr. Mattison met them. "What have you found? Any sign of him?"

"No, sir," Jack said. "But Will saw him go aloft."

Mattison stared out to sea. He had several days' worth of stubble on his chin. The whiskers were gray, though Mattison was probably not much more than thirty-five.

"You're right," Mattison said suddenly. "They were having trouble furling the sails." He turned to the sailors who were still resting on deck. "Did anyone see Wesson come off the ropes?" he yelled.

They stared vacantly at each other. Most denied having seen him aloft, but several remembered him moving around clumsily.

"He must have fallen," Nathaniel said, voicing the thought that no one had been willing to say out loud.

Will looked from one sunburned face to the other, realizing suddenly that the man clinging with one hand to the ropes on the top yard had been Wesson. "He was up there on the top yard," he said quietly. "You saw him, Blue. You called him a fool. Holding on with one arm, he was."

"You're right, lad. God have mercy."

The men were silent as the truth hit home. Wesson had plunged to his death in the sea.

That night Mr. Mattison appointed a light watch so that more men could sleep. Will and Jack lay in their bunks. Jack leaned over and whispered, "I'll bet you're glad it was Wesson."

"Shut up!" Will said.

"I was only joking. But after the things he said about you—that you were a thief—I thought you might be glad."

Will rolled onto his side and pulled the blanket over his head, shutting out Jack's voice.

Jack's words echoed through Will's dreams that night. And the next day, he found that they were shared by many of the men. Will hardened his heart against their accusing stares. When the captain came out midmorning, his black hat in hand, and called the men together, Will stood on the fringe.

"Our Father," the captain began, "have mercy on us. We are poor sinners, deserving nothing but your wrath and curse. Remove your heavy hand of judgment from us. Take away our sin." There was a restless stirring, but the captain seemed indifferent to it. "Let the death of poor Wesson be a warning to us all," he went on, his voice so low that it seemed to reach to the very depths of Will's soul. "Let us consider the length of our days and seek refuge in our only secure port, the Lord Jesus Christ. Amen." There were a few muttered "amens" before the crew drifted away.

Will felt strangely stirred by the captain's words, which he didn't really understand. He was anxious to reach land and almost relieved when Nathaniel shoved a bucket at him and ordered him back to work.

He'd been working steadily for an hour when Mr. Mattison caught up with him. "It's always hard when we lose a man. It's like a hole in our number that we cannot fill."

Will didn't know what to say, and so he said nothing. He had been thinking about Wesson all morning—half expecting him to jump out and accuse Will again. It would have eased the guilt, he figured.

Mattison scratched the whiskers on his chin. He still had not shaved. "I've known Wesson since he was your age. He started as a boy like you. Been on the captain's ships all that time," he added.

"What about his family?"

"Recently took a wife in Bristol—but he never was one to spend much time on shore. Sailed every time the ship left port. Not much of a life for a shore-bound wife."

"What'll happen to her?" Will asked.

"We'll send a letter with the first ship. Plus some money from the crew and captain."

Will was silent. Then he confessed, "I hated him."

"Hate's a strong word."

"Not too strong for how I felt about him," Will said.

"Do you want to tell me about it?"

Will looked up at the first mate and saw kindness in his eyes. But he didn't know what to say; so he said nothing. After a while Mattison patted him on the back and walked away.

NINE

On the thirty-fifth day of the voyage, five weeks from the day they'd set sail from Southwark, Will heard the cry he'd been waiting for. "Land ho!" The crew rushed on deck, each man wanting to be the first to see with his eyes what the lookout had seen with his telescope from aloft.

Will stared intently across the water, but he could see nothing but gray sky meeting gray water. Signs of land were everywhere, from the gulls swooping overhead to the faraway silhouettes of other ships.

It was an hour more before the first outlines of land appeared. A cheer went up among the men, and even the captain came on deck, leaning heavily on his cane.

"No hard feelings, are there?" Will looked up and saw Jack standing in front of him, holding out his hand. "There's Boston. It's not much when you compare it to London."

"I hate London," Will said.

"They say it's the greatest city in the world."

"Do I care what they say? I've seen nothing but the view from under the table. Scraps is all it has ever given me. But in Boston—aye, a man can make his fortune."

Jack laughed. "P'raps , but I'll take life at sea."

"The sea is fine, but give me dry ground and half a chance, and I'll make my fortune."

"What makes you think you'll fare any better in Boston than you did in London?"

Will shrugged. "It matters not about my father or

mother here. I'm as strong as any lad; so why shouldn't I succeed?"

"Because you have nothing," Jack said matter-of-factly. "And nothing gets you nothing whether in London or Boston."

"But what about my pa?"

"I know what you said about him, but I figure it was all lies."

"We'll see." Will was too happy about seeing land to argue. "I've a feeling that I'll find my pa, and he'll make it all right."

"I hope you're right. I do," Jack said, slapping Will on the back.

Will laughed. "I'll wager that in ten years if we meet, I'll have a fair fortune, and you'll be begging my favors."

Jack laughed good-naturedly and poked Will in the chest. "It's a wager I'll look forward to collecting," he said. "But I'll have to find yer graveyard first. Or p'raps find you in jail."

Will watched enviously as the regular crew left the ship, having been paid by Mr. Mattison. The boy waited impatiently for the first mate to come for him. But it wasn't until all the loose ends had been tended to that Mattison approached, ditty bag in hand.

"I've been thinking about a place for you," he said. "Can you read?"

Will nodded. "Some, though I ain't done that much of it."

"You'll need some work on your grammar and spelling, but I think I know a printer who would take you on. A printer's devil you would be. How does that sound?"

Will shrugged. Strange that he hadn't given much thought to what he'd do once he arrived in Boston, other than to find his father—and that would have to wait.

So the next morning Mr. Mattison and Will left the *Ana Eliza* and stepped onto Long Wharf. Will's legs buckled when he hit solid ground. After months at sea he was not used to the firm ground beneath his rubbery legs. He staggered next to Mattison, who had already regained his land legs.

The waterfront was crowded with shipyards and taverns. Cries of "Buy Lobs" and "Oys, oys" came from hawkers selling lobsters and oysters from their brightly painted carts. Noisy gulls hovered overhead.

"Mr. Mattison!"

Will and the mate looked up and saw Blue hanging out the door of a tavern, a woman on each arm. He raised his tankard in salute and said, "Come and have a drink. The ale is fine."

"Can't do." Mr. Mattison waved back. "We're off to printer Spelman to see about a spot for Will here."

Blue seemed to find the thought amusing. "P'raps he'll make a better printer than sailor."

Will blushed, but the first mate brushed away the comment. "You did fine for your first trip. But you either have the sea in your blood, or you don't. There's no shame in choosing to stay in Boston."

As they walked, Will stared around, eager to learn about this city that would now be his home. It was a small place, and from the look of its buildings, a poor one. There were no grand cathedrals, though church steeples—more than a dozen—towered over the town's other buildings. Most of the buildings were wood, and those were blackened from soot and weather. Wharves—homes to merchants, craftsmen, and tavern keepers—sliced into the sea. Narrow streets, as if drawn by a blind man, came together at odd angles. It was on one of those alleys, Dassett Alley, that William Spelman had a print shop.

Mr. Mattison pushed through the door into a small first-floor room with its large printing press and ink-spattered floors. Wooden cabinets full of trays of metal type lined the walls. Large windows lit the room, which smelled strongly of ink. A barrel-chested man who looked as though he'd spent time behind a plow looked up from the table where he was arranging type.

"Ah, Mattison. I heard the *Ana Eliza* had made port. Fair voyage?"

"For the most part, aye. Though a sudden squall cost us a sailor."

"I'm sorry to hear that," the printer said. "Excuse me if I don't stop. I'm working on a rush order—it's promised for this afternoon, and I have no help."

"I can talk while you work if it won't bother you."

"Go ahead." The printer continued searching for the bits of type in the tray that sat on the table. Meanwhile, Will wandered around the shop, reading the various signs that hung on the wall.

"I'm looking for a place for this boy," Mattison said. "We gave him passage, and now he needs to be apprenticed. He reads, though not well, but he's bright and teachable. Do you need help?"

"Need help? I always need help," the printer said, standing up and arching his back as though needing to rid it of a crick. "Look around you. All those trays of type haven't been sorted for weeks. Every time I need to do a job, it's harder and harder to find the type because it is so out of sorts. And look at this floor. I can't tell you the last time it was scrubbed. Aye, I could use help."

"Will you take the boy on?"

The printer eyed Will uneasily. "Now that's a different question, isn't it? I need help, I readily confess. But can I afford it? That is the question. I've never been through a worse season in Boston. These past few years have taken their toll. Every merchant in town is in debt, and the mechanics—those of us who work with our hands—are struggling to survive."

"But surely you eat," Mattison said with a laugh. "It's not as though you must pay him with coin. You must only promise to feed him as you feed yourself—and teach him your trade. A fair deal, I would think."

Spelman shrugged his shoulders. "You could be right," he said. "There, I've finished here. Let's walk down to the Cromwell. I can think better over a glass."

Will followed the two men out of the print shop. Will knew when they reached the tavern by the sign—a portrait on wood of Oliver Cromwell that hung so low over the doorway that both men had to duck in order to enter.

"No one but Whigs in here." Spelman laughed when he saw a look of dismay cross Mattison's face. "The sign is a way we judge our friends and foes. There are some who won't bow before Mr. Cromwell."

Will felt invisible as the men discussed his future. Spelman never sat still. His fingers drummed on the table, and he cast frequent glances at the clock but not at Will. He seemed in a hurry to leave, and Will had given up hope of landing a job. But then the printer slapped the table and said, "Fine. I'll take him on. And if he proves to be a featherbedder, you'll owe me, Mattison."

Mattison raised his brow. "A hard bargain. Room and board and seven years' service—I don't think you'll be disappointed. One more thing," the first mate said apologetically. "He brings nothing but what he wears on his back."

"That will hardly do," Spelman said with a sudden smile at Will. "No printer's devil of mine will dress like a sailor. But clothes will be no problem. My sister should be able to dress him." He jumped suddenly to his feet when he saw the time on the wall clock. "I must get back to the shop. You take the boy over to my sister's house on Bishop's Alley. You can't miss it—the frame house with the green shutters. Tell her that I sent you and that she should make room for the boy. I'll explain all at supper."

Mr. Mattison rose and signaled Will to get up also. "Thank you, William. I know the boy is grateful for the opportunity."

After shaking hands, Spelman swept out of the room like a whirlwind, sucking the tavern dry of its recent energy. Will and Mattison followed more slowly behind him. "What do you think of him?" Mattison asked.

"He seems fine," Will said. "A bit jumpy perhaps."

Mattison laughed. "That's putting it mildly. But you'll find him a fair man."

TEN

The Simpson house was a two-story saltbox structure with a big garden to the side. The house had a tired look about it. Its clapboards were gray from the weather, and the dark green shutters sagged sadly. Will followed Mr. Mattison up the walk. A tall, sturdy boy about Will's age yanked the door open. His green eyes brightened when he recognized Mr. Mattison.

"Ah, Mr. Mattison. Mother will be glad to see you. Last time you paid a visit, you brought her some tea, and she has been singing your praises ever since. Will you be staying with us?"

"It's good to see you as well, Samuel. You look as though you've grown and put on muscle. You'll be ready to go to sea soon."

The boy scowled. "You'll have to convince Mother," he said. "She's not keen on the sailing life—especially now that father's gone."

"I heard about your father. I'm sorry. Smallpox?"

Samuel kicked at the doorstep, trying to control his emotions. "Drowned."

Behind him a woman's voice called, "Samuel, who's that at the door?"

Samuel blushed and opened the door wider and motioned Mattison and Will to follow him inside. "Now Mother will be scolding me for my bad manners. Mebbe you could tell her how I need to go off to sea. I can't seem to do anything right here."

Mr. Mattison clapped a hand on the boy's back. "You must be patient with your mother," he urged. "She'll change her mind in time. By the way, this is Will Northaway. He's going to be apprenticed to your Uncle William at the print shop."

Samuel eyed Will curiously, taking in his suntanned face and the scar on his cheek. "Have you been to sea?" he asked eagerly.

When Will nodded, a look of disgust came over his face. "It's just not fair," he wailed. "Was it wonderful?"

"It was all right," Will said. "But I was glad to see land."

"Not me," Samuel bragged. The sound of footsteps behind him silenced him. A tall, thin woman, wearing a starched cap that could not hide a tired face, appeared from the kitchen. Her face brightened when she saw Mattison. "John," she said, "we've been waiting for the *Ana Eliza*. It's good to see you."

"I'm sorry to hear about George's death," Mattison said softly. "He was a good man."

"That he was. But God has been teaching us the riches of his grace. And we are thankful that he left us this fine house. By renting rooms I'm able to provide for the boys. My brother lives here now as well."

"Yes, well, that's why I'm here actually. I've brought along your brother's new apprentice. His name is Will Northaway."

Will nodded shyly.

"He asked you to find a place for him. Perhaps he could share with Samuel. William also said you would have some clothes for the boy, for he has brought nothing with him."

Mrs. Simpson regarded Will with solemn gray eyes. She twisted the thin gold band on her left hand nervously. "I don't know," she said slowly. "William should have spoken to me."

"Come, Deborah. Let's speak in the garden." Will watched as Mr. Mattison led the woman out into the well-tended garden.

Samuel pulled the boy aside. "She always takes a bit of convincing, but she'll take you in. She adores Uncle William. Besides, she'll feel sorry for you."

Will jerked his arm away. "I don't need anyone feeling sorry for me," he snapped.

"I didn't mean anything by it. She just mothers everyone who needs mothering, including some like me who are getting too old for it."

Suddenly the quiet of the front parlor, where Will and Samuel stood, was broken as two noisy boys tumbled through the door. "The twins," Samuel said apologetically. Two red-faced little boys rushed into the room, poking at each other as they ran. Samuel grabbed one in each hand and lifted them off the floor by their shirt collars. "What's wrong with you two?" he growled. "Don't you know we have company? Mr. Mattison is here."

The bickering turned to squeals of delight. "Let us down. Where is he?"

"I won't put you down until you promise to stop fighting. Mother already looks worn out. This is Will Northaway. He just sailed over from England. If you're good, mebbe he'll tell you lots of stories about sailing ships."

The boys stopped kicking, and their brother set them down. They eyed Will shyly from the safety of Samuel's back, peeking around their brother and giggling when Will met their stares.

"He looks like a pirate," Tommy said.

"Does not," Jacob answered. "He doesn't have a patch."

"Not all pirates have patches," Tommy said knowingly.

"Look at the scar." Tommy had been getting braver, inching forward until he stood in front of Will. "Did a pirate slash you with his sword?" he asked.

Will smiled and shook his head. "Not quite."

"I told you he'd have lots of stories," Samuel interrupted. "Just not right now. If you go out in the garden, you'll find Mr. Mattison. They've been out there long enough. I'm hungry."

Will realized that he was hungry too. So he was glad when Mrs. Simpson reappeared and announced it was time to eat. She invited Mr. Mattison to stay, but he shook his head. "I have much to attend to on the ship. I've been away long enough as it is. Will, see me off?"

Will followed the first mate out the door. The older man turned to him and said, "I've done what I can for you. It's what Mr. Fenlaw asked me to do. Now it's up to you." Will nodded as the first mate continued, "I know you had difficulties with Wesson—and I don't know the cause. Nor do I want to know. But you have a fresh start here. I hope you'll take advantage of it."

Will's throat tightened. "When will you leave Boston?" he asked.

"It'll be several weeks. We must unload the cargo and take on more."

"Will I see you again?"

"I'll try to stop by the print shop before we set sail." Mattison shook the boy's hand. "God be with you," he said solemnly.

Will watched through misty eyes until Mattison was out of sight. Then he slipped into the garden, not wanting to run into Samuel or the twins right then. He hadn't been there more than two minutes when he heard Samuel calling him to lunch. With a sigh, he entered the Simpsons' house, smiling as a wail came from the back of the house. He followed the noise until he came to the kitchen. Jacob had spilled milk all over the table. It dripped onto the floor where Tommy was crawling around with a rag trying to wipe it up. Samuel was scolding Jacob, which just made him cry louder, and Mrs. Simpson—who entered the room after Will—glared at her oldest son. Will looked from one Simpson to the other, wishing he could disappear back onto the ship where there were no mothers or little boys.

"Jacob, that's enough of that caterwauling," she said firmly as she bent over and took the sodden rags from Tommy. "Thank you, Tommy, for cleaning up the mess. And you," she said with a disapproving glance at Samuel, "you are old enough to control your temper. It was just a cup of spilled milk."

"But now I'll have no milk in my tea."

"And it wouldn't hurt you to give it up for the sake of peace."

Samuel scowled, and Mrs. Simpson turned her weary face to Will. "We aren't always this noisy," she apologized. "Have a seat here," she added, pointing to a place on the bench next to Samuel.

Will slid into his seat. Jacob, looking miserable, sobbed noisily even after Mrs. Simpson said, "Let us pray." Will wondered if God could hear the prayer over the crying boy.

After lunch Samuel found some clothes for Will, and when Will had changed, Samuel asked his mother if they could go exploring.

"Go ahead," she said. "I have laundry to do, and I want to hang it up while the weather is fair."

"We'll be back for supper," Samuel said.

"No doubt," she agreed with a smile.

ELEVEN

Over the summer, Will and Samuel became friends. Though Samuel was inches taller than Will and pounds heavier, he followed Will around like a puppy, begging for stories. "I've never been anywhere or done anything," he'd complain.

They slept in a little room under the eaves. On hot summer nights, they slept outside under the stars, which were brighter than any stars Will had ever seen in London. There fog and soot had so clouded the air that he could seldom see them.

"Tell me a story," Samuel would beg.

"I'm too tired. Besides, I've told you all my stories," Will would answer.

But somehow, after enough begging, Samuel almost always got his way. Sometimes the little boys would sneak out and listen.

Gradually Will got used to living in a family. At first he didn't like the rules. He'd never known that belching, wiping his nose on his sleeve, and talking with his mouth full were habits to be ashamed of. For a time he was almost afraid to eat, so many were the rules for polite behavior. But soon he learned them.

Getting used to Mrs. Simpson's rules about bathing was more difficult. Once a week, without fail, he was expected to get into a tub of water that sat on the back porch and scrub himself clean. She expected him to take his muddy shoes off and leave them by the door and to change his sheets and towels regularly. When he didn't, she always found him out.

Will rose early each day when the sun was just a rosy glow over the harbor. By first light he made his way to the print shop where he lit the fire, swept the floors, and opened the shutters before his master darkened the doorway.

It was dirty work. Despite the protection of a leather apron, he often came home ink-splattered and stained. His fingers were permanently black, so that he never had to tell anyone what he did for a living.

Spelman was a fair man, but he worked the boy hard. All day long Will sat on a stool, sorting the bits of lead type into trays. By the end of ten hours, his back and eyes ached. Sometimes it got so bad that he could hardly stand straight. And then Master Spelman would look up from his work-table and say, "Why don't you run these pamphlets down to Sam Adams's house on Purchase Street?" Will would look up gratefully from his trays and be out the door before his master could change his mind.

It was on one of those errands that Will first met Sam Adams. Always before, he'd knocked on the door of the shabby little house on Purchase Street, and a housekeeper had taken the pamphlets, scowling at Will as though it was his fault the house's paint was chipped and the front stoop broken. On one visit Will had seen a young boy and a little girl peeking out the window as he came up the walk. But he had never met Sam Adams himself.

One August day under a baking sun, Will trudged the few blocks to Purchase Street, carrying the latest in the endless supply of pamphlets that seemed to come from Sam Adams's pen. It was so hot, and he was so thirsty that he felt he just had to stop and get something to drink. He had a penny in his pocket, which he used to buy a cup of cider at the corner tavern.

He sank gratefully onto the bench and then took a big

gulp of cider. The room was dark and stuffy. Though the windows were open, no breeze blew in, but since it was out of the sun, it was ten degrees cooler inside than outside. Perhaps that explained why so many "mechanics," which is what the craftsmen in Boston were called, had come in for a drink in the middle of the day. Will finished his cider, but he didn't want to go back outside. He absentmindedly opened one of the brochures and began reading.

He only had time to read enough to know it was about unfair taxes when a short man in a shabby suit with frayed cuffs approached him. "Are you William Spelman's apprentice?"

Will shoved the brochure away. "Yessir," he said.

"I'm Sam Adams. I saw the pamphlet you were reading. Is it mine, by any chance?"

Will blushed bright red and guiltily handed over the bundle of pamphlets. "I just stopped to get a drink," he said. "It was hot."

"You're right about that. I thought if these were mine, I'd save you a trip to the house. I need to take them down to the harbor anyway." The hand in which Adams held the pamphlets trembled.

"I didn't mean to read it," Will began to apologize, hoping Adams wouldn't complain to Master Spelman.

"Well, that's what they're for," Adams said. "What did you think of my argument?"

"I didn't have time to read enough of it," Will admitted.

Adams pulled one of the brochures from his hand and thrust it at the boy. "Then take it and read it. You need to know what's going on. P'raps we can talk about it later." Then with a nod, the odd little man disappeared out the door.

The heat crushed the city for a week. Mothers worried

about sickness, and those who could afford it left for higher ground where a breeze might blow away the sickly air that many believed caused smallpox and other diseases. The twins were cranky, and Mrs. Simpson fretted every time they appeared, red-faced and sweating. She was sure they had come down with a fever. Will and Samuel slept outside every night, but there was no relief from the heat.

Finally the sky darkened, and a cold wind blew off the water. Mrs. Simpson looked out over her garden, which had wilted under the relentless sun. "A nor'easter's coming," she said. "Let's pray the men get in safely."

Will saw Samuel's worried expression and knew that both of them were thinking about Mr. Simpson's accident. He'd been overtaken by a sudden storm. Although his boat was washed to shore, his body was never found.

For the next several hours, the boys made sure the house was secure in case the storm was fierce. Samuel milked the cow and led her into the small barn behind the house. Mrs. Simpson asked all the boys to harvest the corn and other vegetables that were ripe. They had just filled a bushel basket with corn when the rain started. The wind picked up and blew the rain sideways, until Will could hardly see to carry the bushel into the cellar.

Thunder boomed, and lightning flashed. Will sat in a chair, trembling. One of the green shutters came undone and began thumping against the window. "Will, would you go and latch it," Mrs. Simpson requested.

Will stared at her as though not really understanding what she had said. She repeated her request, and still the boy stared. "Will," she said again, a bit louder.

He gulped. His hands trembled, and his heart pounded. "I can't," he whispered, ashamed of his fear.

Mrs. Simpson looked at him curiously and then

shrugged. "Samuel, you do it. Quickly before the wind tears it off."

For two days it stormed. The thunder and lightning kept Will in the house. Samuel tended to the cow, and no one went to church. If William Spelman noticed his apprentice's odd behavior, he never mentioned it. No one else did either, though Will once heard Jacob ask, "Why does Will keep pacing around?" Finally, the heart of the storm passed over, and though a steady rain came down, the thunder and lightning ceased.

On Monday morning Will headed off to work. The streets were muddy and full of puddles. Will discovered that someone had left one of the print shop windows partially open. Water stood on the floor, and the wind had managed to blow a stack of paper everywhere. The boy stared guiltily at the mess, sure that Spelman would blame him.

Before he could clean it up, the door swung open, and Master Spelman stood staring at the flooded room. He glared at Will, who stood guiltily by the open window. "Look at this mess," he roared. "There's a good fortune lost in paper. Do I look as though I'm made of money? Aren't times hard enough? We should join the mob of debtors taking over this city."

Will listened to him yell. From experience he knew that Spelman was like a teapot, quick to boil and equally quick to cool down. But looking again at the mess, he wasn't sure that his master would cool down this time. Will knew he could handle a whipping. He'd suffered his share of beatings over the years. But standing in stocks while Samuel laughed at him—that was a punishment he didn't think he could bear.

Spelman stormed back and forth, picking up pieces of wet paper and crumpling them into balls. As he passed his composing table, he slapped it with an open palm.

Will jumped. "I didn't know the window was open," he said.

"Shouldn't you have known? Isn't that part of your job—to clean up here?"

Will nodded miserably. "Yessir."

"Of course it is. And how you could be so foolish as to leave a window open!"

"But I thought all the windows were closed when I left on Friday. You let me leave early—and I checked everything."

Spelman had stopped screaming at least, but he was still pacing around, casting angry glances at the boy. The boy grabbed a mop and began to clean up the water, making sure to keep a wide berth around the printer.

Spelman slumped down onto his stool and stared at an ink blot. "It wasn't your fault, boy," he said wearily, rubbing his eyes with the thumb and forefinger of his right hand. "We had a late meeting here on Friday night. James Otis was smoking that pipe of his, and it was so hot—I remember opening the windows. I thought we'd closed them, but I guess this one got left open."

Will let out his breath slowly. "Should I throw all the paper away?" he asked.

"If it can be rescued, try. But most of it is a loss," the printer replied, shaking his head sadly. "We'll just have to work harder to make up the loss."

Will didn't think it was possible to work harder, but William Spelman slept very little. If he wasn't printing, he was attending meetings, listening to men like Sam Adams and Joseph Warren, a local doctor in town grumbling about the British. Rumors of a stamp tax—a tax on every bit of paper sold in Boston and the rest of the colonies—angered printers and lawyers and just about everyone else. Parliament had agreed to postpone the tax for a year, but that didn't satisfy men like Sam Adams, who talked openly about cutting the ties between England and Boston.

Though William Spelman was more concerned with making money than politics, he knew there was much money to be made by printing broadsides for the patriots. He was happy when his print shop became a central meeting place for those opposed to British taxes. Most afternoons, while Spelman worked at setting type, a group of men would trickle in, eager to hear the latest news from England and the rest of the colonies. Sam Adams came often. So did Paul Revere— a silversmith from the north end.

Will thought it odd to hear the Harvard-educated Adams argue with the younger silversmith, who had little education. Sometimes Joseph Warren joined them. He always had kind words for Will. And from time to time John Hancock, a rich Boston merchant, waddled in. Hancock alone seemed aware of his position, and Will saw that Sam Adams was attentive to him, making sure he was treated respectfully.

Will found excuses to stay in the back when the debating started. He didn't like the raised voices, especially when it was his master doing the yelling. He feared that Spelman would later take his anger out on him. So when Will heard his master's gravelly voice bellow and saw his face turn red, he would slip into the storeroom at the back of the shop.

One day four of the men were discussing the latest rumors from London. A crane-like man with bulging eyes burst into the print shop and began to rage against Sam Adams. Spelman turned bright red and started arguing with the newcomer. Will slipped off his stool and headed for the storeroom, hoping the storm would blow over soon.

But before he could get away, Spelman called, "Are you running away again?"

Will blushed. "I was just checking something," he explained.

"I've seen you slip off like this before. Now why is that?"

Will shrugged. "I thought you were angry."

"Angry? At you? We're just having a conversation." He looked out over his friends and said, "Not one of us wants to lay a hand on you. So stop hiding back there and go fetch us a pitcher of ale. Mr. Otis will pay. Tell Nate at the Cromwell to put it on Mr. Otis's tab."

Will felt all eyes on him. He looked up to see a good-natured grin on Mr. Spelman's face.

His master pulled him aside and whispered, "Look, son, when I'm angry at you, you'll know it. And you have nothing to fear from my hands. It's not my way. So there's no need to go running to the storeroom every time you hear a voice raised." The printer slapped him on the back as he shoved him out the door.

As Will opened the door of the Cromwell, he remembered Mr. Mattison. "Thank you," he whispered. "You placed me with a good master."

TWELVE

Because of Samuel's dream of going off to sea, every Saturday afternoon when the workday was finished, the two boys trekked down to the half-moon-shaped harbor. It bustled with activity. Something new was always happening. Ships brought news from England and other foreign ports. Sailors, flush with shares from a successful voyage, paid the boys to carry their ditty bags or fetch them ale.

The wharves teemed with people trying to get to the shops that were crowded together like teeth. Children who lived in the houses above the shops chased each other while their worried mothers tried to keep an eye on them. And though they were warned repeatedly to be careful of the water, that didn't stop them from jumping in. Several times each summer, an unfortunate daredevil would crack his head on a rock and drown.

One day in early fall when Samuel and Will were tossing rocks off Hancock's Wharf, aiming at the mast of a vessel moored far out in the harbor, they saw Sam Adams coming out of a small shop. "What do you think he's doing?" Will asked.

"That's Paul Revere's shop," Samuel answered. "They're probably plotting about something."

"Plotting? Why do you say that?"

Samuel blushed. "I don't know. That's what Mother calls it. Though what does she know? She says if Uncle William would spend more time printing and less time plotting, we'd have an easier time of it." As soon as the words were out of his mouth, Samuel regretted them. "Please don't tell Uncle William I said that," he begged.

"Why would I do that?" Will asked, still staring curiously after Sam Adams, who was talking to a fisherman unloading his boat. "Samuel," he said, "if you wanted to find someone in Boston—someone who'd been lost for a long time—who would you ask?"

"That's easy. Sam Adams or Paul Revere. They know everyone. Mother says they're busybodies . . ." Again he realized what he'd said, and he blushed. "I guess I'm acting like a busybody too," he admitted. "Anyway, they know everyone."

Adams had just entered a tavern. Will tugged on his friend's arm. "Do you have any money?"

Samuel jiggled his pocket. "A penny," he replied.

"Good. Just enough for some cider. Will you come with me to that tavern? I just saw Mr. Adams go in."

"But why do you want to see old Sam Adams?" Samuel asked.

Will turned, an annoyed expression on his face. "Because you just told me to," he said.

Samuel looked confused as he followed Will into the tavern. Adams had taken a table near the window, and he saw the boys pass by. He turned and beckoned to Will as they entered.

Will tugged on Samuel's arm. "Don't leave me," he said.

"I'm right behind you," the other boy whispered.

Adams was in a good mood. "Sit down, boys. Join me for some chowder?"

The boys exchanged embarrassed looks.

"What's wrong? Are you not hungry?"

Samuel cleared his throat. "We don't have any money," he whispered.

"Oh, that's all. Don't worry. Jack here will put the chowder on my tab."

"And what tab is that, Sam Adams?" Jack, the tavern keeper, scowled as he ladled out the thick chowder into earthenware bowls. "You've never bought a meal here," he said as he thumped the bowls down in front of the boys.

Adams grinned. "Cheer up, Jack. I've brought you two new customers."

"Aye, the same kind you are. Ones without money."

"Isn't that the case for most of Boston? A harder year I don't remember," Adams said sighing. "But your chowder never changes. And we should be grateful for good gifts." He raised his spoon high in salute before turning to the boys. "What brings you down to the waterfront?"

Samuel was quick to speak. "I'm just waiting for my mother to let me go to sea."

Adams nodded. "A worthy calling. And how about you?" he said, looking at Will.

"I'm content at the print shop," the boy answered.

"So you had enough of the sea?"

"Aye. I'm not eager to leave Boston. I think my traveling days are over."

For the next several minutes Mr. Adams talked about politics. When he finished, silence came over the group. Samuel kicked Will under the table.

"Why did you do that?" Will snapped.

"Because you wanted to ask something," Samuel reminded him through gritted teeth.

Will scowled while Adams glanced back and forth between the boys. When Will still didn't speak, Samuel said, "He wants to know if you could find someone."

Will stared at Samuel until the boy shut up.

Adams waited for Will to speak. He checked his watch,

and when the boy still remained quiet, he said, "I must be going soon. How can I help you?"

"It's my father," Will said slowly.

"Your father?"

"Yes. Before I left Southwark, a woman—my mother's friend—told me that my father had come to Boston. She said he left before I was born. Maybe in '51 or '52."

"What's his name?"

"His last name was Northaway, same as mine. I don't know his Christian name."

"Northaway . . ." Adams rolled the name around on his tongue. "I can't think of a Northaway right off hand. Not a common name though." He stood up to go, but when he saw the disappointed look on Will's face, he added, "Don't look so disappointed. I'll inquire around. I'm sure if your father lives in Boston, he won't be hard to find."

By November Will still had learned nothing of his father, and his dreams of a grand meeting had begun to fade. He liked living with the Simpsons and found Mr. Spelman a good master. The weather had changed. Bitter winds blew off the ocean, often bringing cold rains. The trees had lost their brilliant leaves, and winter began to hold the city in its icy grip.

Will and Samuel shivered in their tiny room under the eaves. Cold winds rattled the shutters and seeped through the cracks in the siding. As the temperatures dropped, the risk of fire increased. People built larger fires in their fireplaces and left them unattended at night. More than once Will's sleep was interrupted by chiming church bells calling out firefighters to battle a blaze. Will and Samuel watched the fires burning from the tiny window in their attic room. For Will there was nothing scarier than to see the hungry orange flames licking the night sky.

Almost weekly Doc Warren came into the print shop,

bearing stories of children who had played too close to a fireplace—stories that Mr. Spelman repeated in gory detail to the lively Simpson twins.

But winter brought more than storms and fires. As November 1764 began, Boston crackled with excitement. Pope's Day, November 5, was drawing near. Although hardly anyone remembered why the day was important—a failed Catholic plot to regain control in England more than 100 years earlier— it had become an excuse for street demonstrations and even riots. Samuel could talk of nothing else. Though his mother had declared that neither boy would be allowed out on November 5, Will and Samuel huddled in their bed in the room under the eaves and plotted their escape.

Will soon learned that Samuel had never seen a Pope's Day celebration. The next day at work, Will overheard an interesting conversation. It was raining steadily when Joseph Warren pushed open the door of the print shop. He stood in the doorway, letting the water stream off his coat and onto the wood floor. "It's wicked out there," he said, stomping his feet.

"Well, take your wet things off and come warm yourself by the fire," William Spelman said. Doc Warren hung his coat and tri-corner hat on a peg near the door. He pulled a stool up to the fire and stretched out his long legs until his boots almost touched one of the smoky logs. The smell of wet leather filled the room.

"It would be a blessing if the rain continued all week," he remarked. "I dread this year's Pope's Day more than I have in the past."

The printer looked up from his work. "I'd almost forgotten. What is Ebenezer Mackintosh up to?"

"He's turned the south end men into an army, just

about. He's had them marching up and down on the Green. Now what is the use of that, I ask you? Unless he's looking for trouble."

Spelman scowled. "I only wish we had more constables to keep order."

Will had set down the type he was sorting as he listened. "I don't understand what's going on," he said.

"It's a good thing you don't," growled Spelman.

Doc Warren smiled at his friend, whose face had become an angry red. "William, you must calm down. You'll burst a blood vessel if you aren't careful." Then he turned to Will and explained, "Over the past several years the annual Guy Fawkes celebration has become an excuse for riots. The fools in this town have divided themselves up— north and south—"

"And they stage a street riot," Spelman interrupted.

"Well, it didn't start that way. Both sides make an image of the pope, and they used to have some harmless fun parading their images throughout the city. At the end of the night they burned the two dummies in a giant bonfire. Harmless fun in the dark days of winter."

"You're too soft on them," Spelman insisted, his face growing dangerously red again. "Haven't they turned their harmless fun into street battles the past several years? Tell the boy about all the split heads and broken bones you fix the next day."

The doctor nodded soberly. "It's too true. Ever since the shoemaker, Ebenezer Mackintosh, began organizing our south end men, the fighting has grown worse. You're right about that, Spelman."

The printer nodded, calming down somewhat now that his friend had agreed with him.

The doctor got up reluctantly. "You know, Spelman,

you can criticize the men who go out on Pope's Night. But it might be better if we could channel that energy into something useful. Perhaps those men just need new leadership."

"Mackintosh won't step aside unless he's forced to," Spelman grumbled as Warren opened the door, letting in a whoosh of cold, wet air.

THIRTEEN

It was late when William Spelman came home. Supper had been served, and Mrs. Simpson left a pot of stew hanging over the fire for him. The boys were whispering under their blanket when they heard him come in, talking in the loud voice that meant he'd been drinking ale at the Cromwell. The rain had finally stopped. Frost covered the windows and whitened the rooftops and the remains of the garden.

At first the boys paid little attention to the raised voices, but when they heard Mrs. Simpson's weepy voice saying, "Must you go?" their ears perked up.

"Shh!" Samuel hissed. "It sounds like Mother is crying."

"What do you think your uncle said?"

"If you'd stop talking, maybe we could hear."

They strained to hear the voices, which had faded as the adults moved into the kitchen.

"I can't hear a thing," Samuel said. "I'm going down and find out."

"Then I'm going with you," Will announced.

William Spelman turned when the boys entered the room. His face was solemn. Mrs. Simpson tried to turn away, but not before the boys saw her tear-swollen face.

"What's wrong, Mother?"

She sat down wearily at the long trestle table, twisting a handkerchief between her hands. "Uncle William is going to Lexington. Uncle Nathan is very sick—and there's no one else to go."

"But don't you want him to go? That's father's brother."

"Of course I want him to go," she said, quietly wiping away a tear. "But it worries me that William might come down with the smallpox . . ." Her lip trembled, and she couldn't go on.

Will stood awkwardly behind Samuel, wishing he'd stayed up in the room under the eaves. Samuel and Mr. Spelman looked as uncomfortable as he felt. Finally the printer said, "We don't even know that he has the smallpox. It might just be the ague. Besides, there's no need to worry. Didn't I have an inoculation?"

"You did, but we know they don't always take." She spoke bitterly, spitting out the words as if they were foul-tasting.

"Sister, you forget that we are in the hands of a wise God. It's not fitting for you to be so fearful. Now I must go—and I pray that you will let me go without further tears."

She sniffed away a tear and managed a wan smile. "I'm sorry. You're right, of course. I try so hard to trust, but it's hard sometimes for me to see God's kindness."

William Spelman turned to his apprentice. "Will, while I'm gone, I leave you under Mrs. Simpson's care. Help Samuel around the house, for there is nothing pressing at the shop. Whatever is there will keep until I return."

Everything that could go wrong seemed to go wrong the morning of November 5. The day was bright and cold. By midmorning the frost had melted, but the air still bit as the boys did the chores. Someone had forgotten to latch the gate to the pigpen, and the sow had gotten out and rooted in the potatoes still in the ground. Will and Samuel chased the ornery pig, finally cornering it a block away.

Mrs. Simpson was short-tempered with the twins, who, sensing her mood, seemed to be more energetic than usual. By noon everyone was snapping at everyone else. So when

Samuel began to beg his mother for permission to go to the Guy Fawkes parade, she finally threw up her hands and told him to do whatever he pleased, as long as he kept out of trouble.

Samuel didn't need any more encouragement. "Come on, Will. Let's go on down to the Green. They'll be putting the finishing touches on the pope."

Will looked back regretfully at Mrs. Simpson, who stared sadly out the window after them. "Don't you feel bad leaving your mother like that?" he asked.

"Nope," Samuel answered. "She said we could go, didn't she? What more do you want?"

"She didn't seem very happy."

"But she didn't say no," Samuel insisted.

In order to reach the Green, they had to pass down Purchase Street. As they walked by Sam Adams's rundown house, he came out. He called Will over.

Samuel regarded his friend impatiently.

"Go on ahead," Will said. "I'll catch up with you."

Samuel looked relieved and waved a quick good-bye.

Adams watched Samuel hurry down the street. "Your friend is eager for the festivities?"

"Samuel is always eager for excitement," Will said, watching his friend until he disappeared around a corner.

"And you? Are you going out tonight?"

Will shrugged guiltily. "I promised Samuel I'd meet him," he replied. "And you?"

"No. I'll be at home," Adams said. "You be careful. For mark my words, there'll be trouble. Ebenezer Mackintosh will do his best to stir up the crowd. I wish he'd spend more time making shoes and less time rabble-rousing."

"Mrs. Simpson said we could go," Will said, feeling as though he had to explain his decision.

"Then I pray you be wise," Adams said seriously. "There will be many good men there. But there will also be trouble. It seems to me that this town is lurching toward either liberty or license, and Mackintosh fans the flames of license, encouraging drunkenness and lawlessness. Too many of our citizens would rather not work and are happy to follow him. It worries me."

"We'll be careful. We promised Mrs. Simpson to stay out of trouble."

Adams nodded before remembering that he had called the boy over for a reason. "I just remembered, I found out something about a Northaway."

"My father?" Will asked, grabbing Adams's wrist in his excitement.

"Now I don't know if it's your father. But I've been asking around—as I said I would. And there is a George Northaway who works . . . on the waterfront . . ."

Will was so excited at the information that he didn't notice the unhappy look on Sam Adams's face. All he could think of was the grand meeting with his father that he had dreamed about for so long. "Can I meet him?"

"Slow down. We don't yet know that he's your father," Adams said slowly. "Besides, you may be expecting too much of this man."

"Is he from Boston?" Will asked.

"Well, he's been here for years," Adams began. The boy felt his hopes dip, but then Adams continued, "It's been at least ten years, of that I'm certain. But I'm just as certain that he's not native to these parts."

"Then it could be him." Once again Will felt a surge of excitement. "Where will I find him?"

"Slow down, son," Adams urged.

"But how can I slow down if it might be my father?"

"Even if it is, he may not be the sort of man you're expecting."

Will barely heard the older man's words. His mind was racing ahead, thinking about what he'd say when he met George Northaway. He felt a tug on his arm.

"Did you hear what I said?" Adams asked.

Will shook his head. "I'm sorry. I wasn't listening."

"Sometimes it's best to leave dreams alone."

It took a few moments for the words to sink in. Then Will said, "What do you mean?"

"I mean that you should not get your hopes up. The George Northaway I'm talking about—"

"I don't want to hear it," Will half shouted. "Just tell me where to find him."

The older man hesitated until he saw the look of determination on the boy's face. "I fear you'll be disappointed," he warned.

"That may be," the boy answered, "but I must find out."

"Then try Phillips Rope Walk first. You'll find it on Griffin Wharf."

Will forgot all about meeting Samuel in his eagerness to get to the rope walk building. He trotted down the narrow streets until he reached the harbor where he found Griffin Wharf close to Windmill Point. Will found the rope walk easily. It was a long, narrow building with high windows on the walls. The wharf was strangely quiet as though the workers had all taken the day off. He hesitated in front of the building, trying to tamp down his excitement.

Finally he summoned the courage to cross the street and knock on the door. "Come in!" a voice shouted.

Will shoved open the door and stood hesitantly in the entrance. The room was empty except for the enormous spools of rope that dotted the factory. The floor was dusty with rope fiber. A man sat half-hidden behind a cluttered desk. He looked up and scowled when he saw Will.

"What do you want?" he growled, about as friendly as a bulldog. His sagging cheeks trembled as he peered over his half-glasses at the boy.

"I was looking for a man called George Northaway," Will replied.

The man's scowl deepened, and he rose halfway from his chair. "What do you want with that no-account fellow?"

Will felt the hairs on his neck prickle. "Sam Adams said you might know where he is."

"He did, did he? Well, tell Adams that I haven't seen him for weeks, not since payday—and I'm sure he's drinking up every cent that I gave him." The man thumped his fleshy fist upon the desk, causing a pulley to bounce and skitter to the floor.

Will took a step backwards and tried again. "Do you know where he lives?"

"What do I care?" the man said, slumping down wearily. "My best guess would be to look for Ebenezer Mackintosh. You find him, and you'll find George Northaway."

"Thank you," Will said, turning to go.

"I doubt you'll thank me once you meet him," the man muttered as Will shut the door behind him.

FOURTEEN

Church bells tolled as Will stumbled out onto the street. He could think of nothing but the man's words; Samuel was all but forgotten. The sky faded, melting from rose to blue, but Will was only vaguely aware of it. Around him men and boys pushed past in a rush to some unknown destination. He let himself be carried along, like a stick on the surface of a brook, carried by invisible currents.

"Move along!" He felt a hand on his shoulder and turned in time to see a burly fellow carrying a heavy leather satchel push past him. "Get out of the way. Can't you see we're in a hurry here?"

Will moved out of the way, but not before another man stepped on the heel of his boot. "Pay attention. You're in the way. Now move along."

It was easier to fall in step with the crowd than fight against it; so Will quickened his pace to keep up. They were mostly working men, judging from their clothes and the odors that followed them—dock workers, fishermen, rope makers. They poured out of taverns and shops until the streets were full.

"It's near time," one said.

"Time for what?" Will asked.

"Are you daft? It's Guy Fawkes." The man scowled as he passed by.

When he reached a crossroad, Will ducked into a doorway to get out of the wind and considered what to do. It was dark, with only a cusp of the moon lighting the night sky.

Slivers of light escaped from shuttered windows. Light from a street lantern puddled on the ground. Will listened as the voices faded. He was in an unfamiliar neighborhood. From the corner of his eye he saw scared faces peering out from half-shuttered windows. Behind him a child scampered across the street, looking for coins that might have fallen from a passing pocket.

Will blew on his hands to warm them. He knew he should go home. Only trouble would befriend him this night, but the desire to find his father overcame any fear. He looked down the street where he could still make out the backs of the stragglers. Shaking off his doubts, he ran to catch up with them.

It was a rowdy, drunken, swaggering group of men, and the closer it drew to the Liberty Tree, the louder it grew. By the time it reached the corner of Orange, Essex, and Newberry Streets, Will had put off any doubts about being there. Someone handed him a clay bowl. He took a swig from it and felt the ale bite the back of his throat. He took another swig and felt it warm its way to his belly.

He elbowed his way to the center of the crowd, full of good feelings about the men who surrounded him. Their drunken speeches seemed profound, and Will felt himself lucky to be part of such a group. He watched as several fellows in front of him put the finishing touches on a dummy of the pope. It was funny to watch, for the men were obviously drunk, and they had trouble climbing on the wagon where the figure was enthroned. The pope was a showy figure, much bigger than a man. It tilted unsteadily so that its crown threatened to fall from its large curled and powdered wig.

One man was trying to button the dummy's vest, but he couldn't stretch the fabric across its enormous stuffed belly. His helpers managed to pull the fabric tight, but they buttoned it unevenly.

Will giggled. "You've buttoned it all wrong," he jeered.

After a string of curses the two men leaned away to study their handiwork. One of them, a short man with black stubble on his cheeks, began to laugh. He chucked his friend on the head and said, "You're a lout, Smith. Let the lad fix the vest, for we can't have a pope with his vest out of line, now can we?"

Smith muttered something under his breath and hopped down from the wagon. He turned to Will and said, "Do a better job if you can. I'm dry and need a drink."

Will watched as he staggered off, his red hair looking like a blaze in the lantern light. Then Will easily climbed on the wagon. "You hold it closed, and I'll button," he said to the first man. They struggled for a minute but soon had the garment hooked.

"What are you going to do about the leaning?" Will asked. "He's likely to tumble to the street."

"That's not my concern," the man said. "Ain't we done enough? Let Mackintosh worry about it. Let's you and me fetch another ale."

Will shook his head. He already felt a bit lightheaded from the bowl he'd had. "Who's Mackintosh?" he asked.

"You must be new to Boston," the man said, eyeing the boy. "Everyone knows Mackintosh. Meanest cur this side of the ocean." He looked around until he spotted a small man, red-haired and freckled, pacing back and forth. The little man was grabbing some men by the arms and slapping others on the back, barking commands as if he were a general ordering his troops. "That's Mackintosh," he said, pointing. "I'd stay out of his way unless you have a hankering to be his punching bag."

It was clear to Will that Mackintosh was the leader. He seemed to be the only one who wasn't drunk. Even when the men began singing, making up verses on the fly, Mackintosh kept a stern eye on the wagon.

Will tried to see the wagon through the shoemaker's eyes. Something clearly displeased him, for he never smiled. The pope still leaned dangerously, like a baby about to tumble on its face. Will knew the dummy would fall over at the first pothole if someone didn't do something to stiffen its back. He found a piece of lumber on the ground and carried it over to the wagon. He was just about to stuff it under the pope's shirt when he heard someone yell, "Northaway!"

Will turned around to see who was yelling at him. Immediately he saw that Mackintosh was doing the yelling but wasn't looking at him. The leader was staring at a stocky man with lank yellow hair that hung in greasy clumps to his shoulders. The man was in the midst of hoisting a tankard when his name rang out again. At once he lowered the tankard and turned to look at Mackintosh. In the lantern light his face looked yellow, as though he was sick. It was gaunt and covered by several days' growth of whiskers.

Will watched as Northaway muttered something to the man next to him. The stocky man deliberately took another swig of ale and slowly wiped his mouth on the sleeve of his shirt before lurching toward Mackintosh. He stopped when he was about two feet away from the shoemaker, as though wanting to keep a cushion between them, but it wasn't far enough. Mackintosh reached out and grabbed him by the vest, jerking him so that the ale sloshed out of his glass and onto his boots.

Will waited to see what the man named Northaway would do. The boy cringed as he heard Mackintosh deliver a tongue-lashing, worse than anything Will had received on the ship. The yellow-haired man stood like a cowed puppy, letting the words pour down on him. Will clenched his fists, for as soon as he'd heard the name Northaway, he'd begun to think of the yellow-haired man as his father. It was silly perhaps. There may have been other men in Boston by that name. But there was something about this man that was familiar. The shape of his body, the turn of his nose, the set of his eyes. It was painful for Will to watch his father's shame.

When Mackintosh tired of his scolding, Northaway looked up and caught Will staring at him. "What are you staring at?" he spat.

Will swallowed hard and tried to pry his tongue loose. "Is your name Northaway?" he asked.

"So it is, and what's it to you?" Northaway stepped forward, his hands balled into fists.

"I don't mean any trouble," Will said, backing away. "I just wondered if you came from Southwark?"

"Who are you?" Northaway grabbed Will by the coat and leaned so close the boy could feel warm, sour breath on his cheek. "I don't like people asking questions about my past."

"I don't mean you any harm," Will said, trying to pull away. "It's just that my name is Northaway. I thought we might be related."

He felt the grip on his coat relax. A knowing smirk crept across Northaway's face. "So you've come looking for money?" His companions laughed.

Will took a deep breath as he gathered his thoughts. This conversation wasn't going the way he had imagined it. He looked up into the scruffy face of the man he knew to be his father and said, "I thought you might be my pa."

"Your pa?" the older man muttered, eyeing Will doubt-fully. He poked the boy in the shoulder and raised his glass in a toast. "Hey," he sneered. "The boy thinks I may be his pa. What do you think? Is he a chip off the old block?" His eyes, blurry from drink, mocked Will. Northaway's friends raised their glasses.

Will let their cheers and jeers fall on his shoulders until the joke died.

Finally his father turned back to him. He belched and said, "Tell me your name again."

"Will Northaway," the boy whispered.

"Let's see if I can guess your story." George Northaway slurred his words together. "Your ma—was she Lizzie, Nellie? Oh, what does it matter? She said go to America and find your father, George Northaway. P'raps he's rich."

"It wasn't at all like that," Will cried angrily. "If you'd stayed in Southwark, you'd know that she died—my ma. All alone with nothing. I've been taking care of myself for years—without you. And I don't need you now." He stalked away, clenching his fists so tightly that his fingernails dug into the palms of his hands. He was determined not to cry. "Worthless swine," he muttered.

Before he knew it, he felt a fist tear into his side. He stumbled to the ground and looked up in time to see George Northaway ready to take another punch at him. It was at that moment, however, that Mackintosh chose to order the pope's wagon forward. Northaway grabbed Will. "It ain't right for a boy to speak that way to a man who might be his pa. Where's your respect?"

Will bit back the sharp reply.

The older Northaway wiped his nose. "If you're my boy, grab onto the wagon."

Will threw himself behind the wagon as the procession wove through narrow alleys and onto broader streets. Bystanders, many wearing pointed dunce caps, lined the route, clapping and chanting and joining in the lusty singing. Drums beat a tattoo. It was a happy crowd, and Will wondered why his master had been so set against the celebration.

Will watched George Northaway from the corner of his eye. The older man was drinking ale with one hand and holding onto the wagon with the other. Sometimes the wagon got hung up on a rut, and then the men in front would turn and scowl at his father. "Too drunk to push, Northaway?"

Will saw his father's feet stumble. He seemed to be using the wagon to keep upright. The boy poked his father on the arm. "Come on, pa," he said, looking sideways at the older man to see how he took being called "pa." "I'll help you push, but you have to hang on."

"Tha's a good boy," George Northaway mumbled. The wagon finally reached the bridge over Mill Pond, the unofficial border between the city's North End and South End. Mackintosh climbed aboard and began to address the crowd, which had dwindled but was getting rowdy.

"Save your fighting for the North End pope," the leader cried.

"Aye, save it," the crowd responded.

Mackintosh waited for the shouts to die down. Then he yelled, "Are you with me?"

"Aye!" the crowd replied.

"Through hell and back?" he demanded.

"To the devil's home itself."

"And what of the North End pope?"

"Death to the North End pope! There's only one pope in Boston."

The air was electric. Will glanced at George Northaway, who had gained a second wind. His father raised his fist and yelled, "Death to the North End pope." The words hung like a challenge in the air.

Will hesitated only an instant before joining his voice to his father's. He pumped his fist in the air and yelled, "Death to the North End pope!"

It was as though a dam had broken. His father hugged him and thrust his glass at him. "For courage," he said, watching with satisfaction as the boy drank it down. "You're a Southsider now," he said proudly, slapping his son on the back. Then he grabbed back the ale and held it up in the air for all to see. "Meet my son, Will Northaway."

Mackintosh hopped off the wagon, and it began to roll forward across the narrow bridge, followed by its shouting defenders. Every time they yelled, their chants were met by equally loud bellows from the North End crowd.

Once across the bridge, the Southenders abandoned the wagon and grabbed rocks and bricks and bits of paving stones. By the time the other wagon came into view, Mackintosh's men had formed a long battle line. They began pelting the other side with rocks.

Will hadn't expected this development. He stared at his father with bewilderment. "What're you doing?" He grabbed his father by the arm. "Someone will get hurt."

The older man shook him off. "Let go, boy. It's war. People get hurt in wars."

"War against whom?" Will demanded.

"The North End pope—and those who fight under his flag," his father answered. He crouched behind a hay wagon. Will knelt beside him.

"That makes no sense," Will argued. "Aren't you all from Boston? Tomorrow won't you be working together? How can you go after them with rocks and bricks?"

"Because tonight they've sided with the devil. Now if you won't join in, get away from me. I called you my son, but if you won't fight with me, you're no relation of mine, and you might as well go back to your mother."

Will grabbed his father's upraised arm and shook the rock loose. "Look at me," he shouted. "My ma is dead. Dead. Did you hear me?"

For a moment the older man paused, and his expression softened as though he felt pity—or maybe even love for his son. In that instant Will caught a glimpse of his father as a young man, before time and drink had left their marks. But just as quickly the expression hardened, and the yellow-haired man said, "If you're truly my son, follow me."

Will shook his head, but then a piece of brick flew across the street, striking him in the chest. Without thinking, he bent over and picked up a rock. The next thing he knew, he had hurled it across the street.

His father cleared his throat. "Good throw, son," he said, a satisfied look on his face. "Now arm yourself. A man has to defend himself."

The no-man's-land between the two sides was soon full of flying objects. Will joined heartily in the fighting, stopping only to refill his pockets with rocks. When a vigorous attack came against the South End pope, George Northaway, followed by a small army of followers, dashed to its protection, hurling rocks at the attackers and forcing them back.

Will watched his father with pride, admiring the reckless courage that carried him to the middle of the battle. Will ran to join them. But he hadn't gone more than two steps when a rock hit him on the arm, and another nicked his ear. Confused, he looked around, wondering where the stones were coming from. He hadn't seen either one coming.

"Get back," his father shouted.

Will shook his head. He'd be like his father, out in the thick of it. Just then a brick about the size of a fist came sailing through the air and hit the boy on the forehead, knocking him to the cobblestone street. He lay motionless for several minutes while the battle raged around him.

When his head cleared, he staggered to his feet, only to discover that the battle had moved down the block. Will felt a trickle of warm blood on his forehead. His head pounded, and the glamour of battle had faded; he wanted only to find his father and go home. Surely they had fought enough. He caught sight of the two wagons first. Each was surrounded by a small platoon of fighters charged with protecting the popes.

From time to time, one side or the other would stage an attack against the enemy's pope, but neither side had been able to knock the figures to the ground. Will watched the battle from the sidelines, trying to catch a glimpse of his father or Samuel. Then he saw his father step behind a wagon. He and some others pushed the South End wagon like a battering ram toward the enemy wagon. Soon it was rolling on its own, picking up speed as it lumbered out of control toward the other wagon. Suddenly a little boy, no more than five, stumbled into the street in front of the oncoming wagon.

Though everyone saw his danger, events happened too quickly. The wagon rocketed toward the enemy side. The boy looked up to see it barreling down on him. He cried out, "Mama," before the wagon knocked him to the ground, crushing him under its wheels.

For an instant there was shocked silence, then murmured excuses. As the North Enders stopped to investigate, Mackintosh ordered his men to capture the enemy pope. Once he had it in hand, he ordered his men back over the bridge, where they quickly broke ranks and ran as though the devil was on their tails.

George Northaway spotted Will. "Come on, lad. There's no time to wait."

"How can you go?" Will demanded.

"It's not my business—or yours," his father said, casting nervous glances back at Mackintosh.

"I won't just walk away," Will said, shaking his head.

"You'll do as your father tells you," the older man said angrily, whacking the boy across his injured ear.

Will twisted away. "I'd rather have no pa than one like you," he said, his voice cracking.

"Fool!" George Northaway spat. He turned and trotted clumsily after the wagon, leaving Will watching through tear-blurred eyes. Only when his father was out of sight did he turn back to the small crowd of men who had gathered around the small, crumpled body. A weeping woman pushed her way through the crowd. "Is it Ethan?" she cried. "Ethan Brown?"

The men stared shamefacedly at the pavement as the woman knelt by the limp body. "Ethan, Ethan," she wept.

Will didn't wait to hear any more. He backed uneasily away from the scene, eager to put distance between himself and the dead boy. When he reached the bridge, he turned and ran home, where he found Samuel sitting outside the house waiting for him.

"What happened to you?" Samuel asked. "Where were you?"

Will shook his head. "I don't want to talk about it. Leave me alone. I'm tired and going to bed."

FIFTEEN

For the next several weeks the papers were full of news about the "Guy Fawkes riots." Some blamed the trouble on rabble-rousers; others blamed it on the British. Will blamed it on his father. He couldn't shake loose the picture of his father pushing the wagon that hit the Brown child. And he couldn't stamp out the memory of his father's cowardly behavior when he ran away.

The constables arrested Ebenezer Mackintosh for disturbing the peace, but that didn't change anything for Will. He knew his father was guilty. For days the boy was afraid to go out. He skittered around town like a scared mouse, sure he would see his father somewhere or another. But it didn't matter where Master Spelman sent him, he never ran into his father again.

Autumn turned to winter; Christmas came and went. By now the boy's reading came along so well that the printer let him set the type on very simple handbills. In addition to Will's regular tasks, Mr. Spelman often sent him to the forest to bring home dead limbs that could be chopped and stacked for firewood.

The hard work guaranteed that the boy was tired at the end of the day. Most nights his head barely hit the pillow before he fell into a deep sleep. But when the clock struck two or three, when the house was still except for the creaking of the eaves, Will often found himself awake and unable to soothe himself back to sleep. Sometimes the nightmares were so vivid that he woke up screaming at his father—trying to keep him from rolling that wagon.

Samuel would poke him, and then Will would look at his friend as if to ask, "What're you doing here?"

It was a hard winter. January blew in cold, and the city huddled under layers of snow and ice. Storm after storm battered the town, bringing more snow than the boy had ever seen. With the snow came sickness. Smallpox appeared again, as well as flux and ague. Some folks immunized themselves against the pox, but most burned herbs in their fireplaces to keep it away and prayed it would pass. Everyone eyed his neighbor with suspicion, wondering who was carrying fatal germs along with their greetings.

Will was hard at work chopping wood one day when Master Spelman opened the back door and called out to him, "Will Northaway, come in, please!"

Will dried off the ax and hung it on a nail in the shed. He'd learned to take good care of the tools, for he was likely to lose his supper if he didn't. He stomped the snow off his boots and stood in the doorway, waiting for his master to speak.

There was another lad about Will's age in the middle of the room. His cheeks were red with the cold, and his hat was beaded with water where the snow had melted. The boy eyed Will curiously.

"Doc Warren sent this lad to fetch you to him."

"Why?" Will asked, his surprise showing in his voice.

"Didn't say. Just begged me to give you leave for several hours, saying that he would explain all later."

Will looked up at his master. It was just past noon, and Will knew that the printer would hate to lose half a day's labor, for it was likely that several hours would stretch until evening. His master was clearly torn—needing the boy's time but not wanting to offend Doc Warren, who wouldn't have asked for Will without good reason.

Spelman's cheek pulsed with irritation. "I'll give you leave," he said grudgingly. "But see you don't abuse it. The minute he's finished with you, come back here. Or I'll have a piece of you."

Will nodded his agreement and followed the other boy out the door. The lad was in no great hurry to get back. He stopped now and again to pick up a handful of snow to throw at signs and trees as they passed by. Will was content to follow at the boy's pace. They had been walking about fifteen minutes through a part of town that Will did not know when they reached a shabby two-story house, badly in need of a coat of paint. A faint wisp of smoke floated up from the chimney. The boy didn't even bother to knock. He pushed open the door and yelled, "Ma, I'm back. I brought the lad with me."

He held open the door until Will passed and then let it slam behind him. "Take your boots off, for she don't like to scrub."

Will pulled off his boots and waited until a sharp-angled woman poked her head out of the doorway. "Go on back to yer chores," she chided the other lad. Then pointing at Will, she said, "The doctor's in the room there."

Will hesitated until she screeched at him, "Go on. Are you deaf?"

He scurried down the hall, praying she wouldn't reach out one of her bony arms and swat him as he passed. He stuck his head in the room and saw Doc Warren leaning over a bed. The doctor heard the boy and turned in greeting.

"Come in, lad."

Will moved forward a step.

"I've been tending quite a number of folks with the

smallpox. I was down the street when Mrs. Miller—I think you met her as you came in—called me to see this fellow she's been renting a room to.

"Seems he's been sick for months, not able to work and surviving by her kindness. She's been unwilling to put him out on the streets, though he's not paid his rent since Thanksgiving. But last week he took a bad turn, and it's not likely he'll see another day. I gather that he's someone you know. Leastwise, he's been calling your name, and you are the only Will Northaway that I know."

While he was talking, Will had been creeping closer to the doctor until he was standing just behind him. He was hearing the doctor's words but not really getting the sense of them. But somehow he knew that the doctor was talking about his father, George Northaway. He knew that if he raised his eyes, he'd see the familiar face, the same one that had been haunting his dreams all winter.

Part of Will wanted to turn right then and there and race for the door. But instead of running, he found himself standing next to the doctor, looking down on the shell of a man. His father's skin was wafer-thin, crisscrossed by blue veins. The skin around his eyes looked bruised, and the bones in his cheeks threatened to poke through the skin. His breath came in shallow rasps, as though a piece of sandpaper was caught in his windpipe.

"What's wrong with him?" Will whispered.

"Consumption, bloody flux. He's very weak, but he speaks every now and again. It was early this morning that I heard him ask for you. Do you know him?"

Will didn't answer. He gazed down at the ravaged face and felt his anger melt away. All that was left was pity, the sort you'd feel for anyone who was reduced to nothing but skin and the bones that held it up. He felt as though he was looking at a stranger—and Will guessed he was. After all, he'd never really known George Northaway.

Just then his father's eyes fluttered open. At first they darted anxiously about before settling on Will. Seeing the boy seemed to calm the sick man.

The doctor bent over him and whispered, "It's the lad you asked for. He's just come."

The man sighed and closed his eyes. His lips moved silently as though he were talking to himself or someone unseen to any eyes but his. After several moments they fluttered open again. He found Will and reached a frail arm out to him. In a dry, rough voice, which was not much more than a whisper, he said, "I'm sorry, son. I've been a poor father and a poorer man. I would have said nothing . . ." He paused to catch his breath. "I thought it too much to ask," he continued, "but Mrs. Miller urged me. Said it was not too late to beg your forgiveness. I've asked for God's."

When he was done speaking, he sank back onto the mattress, exhausted. His forehead glistened with sweat, and a violent cough overtook him. The doctor covered George Northaway's mouth with a cloth until he had finished coughing. When he pulled it away, Will saw bloody stains on it.

The boy didn't know what he'd expected when he received the message from Doc Warren. But it wasn't a plea for forgiveness from his father on his deathbed. He felt battered by a confusing swirl of emotions: anger, sadness, fear, and pity. He turned away from the sick man and looked at Doc Warren for help.

The doctor finished tending to the patient before hustling the boy out of the room. Mrs. Miller hovered just outside the door. She raised questioning eyes to the doctor.

"I don't think he'll last the night," the doctor said with a shrug. "Keep him comfortable and give him your medicine—as much as he requires, for it can't hurt him, and it might well help."

"Did he make his peace?" she asked.

"I think he did, or as much as God gives it to a man to do. Now it's in the lad's hands, and there's nothing the father can do about that."

She nodded so vigorously that her cap fell forward over her forehead. She muttered under her breath as she pushed it back. "Well, you both can see how much work I have to do. It's not been easy having an extra mouth to feed and no extra money for the food. You'd best be going so that I can get back to my work. Mark will see you out."

"You've done well, Mistress Miller," Doc Warren said. "It can't have been easy, but it was a Samaritan's task. Now come, lad. I'll walk you back to your master's."

The sun was at an angle, casting long shadows on the snow. Will and the doctor trudged along into the wind, barely talking. Only when they turned down Newberry Street did the wind die down, and they could lift their faces from the ground.

Doc Warren turned toward the boy. "Your father, was he?"

Anger erupted from the boy. He spat on the ground. "He was my father in name only. I never laid eyes on him before Guy Fawkes night—and I wish to God that I hadn't then."

The burst of emotion took the doctor by surprise. "Do you want to talk about it?"

"What's to talk about? He was a poor father," Will snapped. "Well, that's not the half of it. He was a poor human being, and he wants me to forgive him. He should go ask Ethan Brown's mother to forgive him . . ." Will's contempt was so strong that it twisted his face almost beyond recognition.

Doc Warren stopped in the middle of the street to let a wagon roll by. Will bent down and picked up a fistful of snow, packed it into an icy ball, and threw it at a tree across the street. It smashed against the trunk, startling a red squirrel skittering up the bark to its nest.

"Those are strong words, son. Are you sure your father deserves them?"

"What would you say to a man who followed Mackintosh as though he was his lord? A man who pushed the wagon that just happened to hit and kill a child? And a man who ran away rather than confessing what he'd done? That's what George Northaway did, and I saw it with my own eyes. And he asks for forgiveness!" The boy spat again as though trying to rid himself of the taste of his father's name.

"Have you told no one this?"

"Who would I tell? Master warned me about Guy Fawkes Day. Never said that I couldn't go, but I knew he didn't like it. Then he was gone, and so I went."

The doctor sighed, which made the boy angry. "Do you think I'm wrong?" he demanded.

"Not wrong, but I see trouble ahead for you," the doctor said bluntly. They were not more than a block from the print shop. Will slowed his pace, wanting to finish this conversation before seeing his master.

The doctor kicked at a ball of ice, sending it sliding into a ditch. "I know a lot about politics and medicine," the doctor said. "Those are my passions. You can ask me my opinion, and I'll not only have one, but I'll have good reasons for it. So I feel a bit awkward here—like maybe you should be talking to the preacher or Sam Adams. But this is how I see it. George Northaway led a miserable life. Not the worst life of anyone I know, but a bad one. He drank too much, he hated responsibility, and he was a coward."

Will had stopped and was listening intently despite the cold.

"But if you're completely honest," the doctor continued, "you're probably not all that much different than your pa."

Will began to protest, but the doctor cut him off. "I don't mean that you're bad because he was bad; I only mean to say that none of us is blameless. P'raps your father should have been tried for the death of that boy. But he's dying. Isn't that punishment enough?"

"So are you saying it doesn't matter what he did? That he can go to heaven because he believed in God on his deathbed? But he abandoned my mother. He wasted his life. He killed that boy. He abandoned . . . me." Will's protest dissolved in sobs.

"I know," Doc Warren said, laying his hand gently on the boy's shoulder. "He's done evil. He deserves more punishment. But Christ died for him, and for me, and . . . for you. I'm saying that before you refuse to forgive him, you might want to examine yourself. A day may come when you will need forgiveness from someone. Do you understand?"

"No!" Will thundered. "That's not right. Wesson on the ship that brought me to Boston was a bad man. He fell off the yardarm and plunged to his death. No last-minute confession. That's the right way: You do wrong; you're punished, now and forever. And you wait and see: I'm not like my father, and I'll never be. I'll do what's right." He stopped, exhausted.

Doc Warren was looking at him intently. "I hope you will," he said, a slight smile playing around his lips. "But it doesn't hurt to remember that a time will come when you'll be needing forgiveness from God. Then you'll be glad that he's the kind of God who forgives even sinners like your father—and you." Doc Warren paused, then said, "Time for you to get back to work," and quickly walked away.

Will was angry, sad, and confused. But before he could collect his thoughts, the print shop door swung open. Master Spelman leaned out and stared at the boy. "It's what I expected when I gave you leave," he said. "Sauntering back here as though you own the shop. I should take a cane to your back. But I guess I'll be merciful this time."

Will hustled into the shop. He slipped on his leather apron and began to sort the bits of type, glad for the ordinariness of the job. The kind printer set a cup of tea next to him and went back to his own work, humming a sea chantey while he worked the press. It was a song that Will remembered from his time at sea.

As he stood listening to the jaunty melody, his memory drifted back to his weeks on board the *Ana Eliza*, and before that to his hard life on the Southwark streets. He thought of Mr. Fenlaw and his family, of Mr. Mattison, and of his father. What did it matter to him if George Northaway was a coward? Hadn't chasing his dream of finding a father been the reason Will left England? Yes, he was Will Northaway, not his father, and right now there was work to do. For once in Will's young life he felt glad to do it.